AROUND CHI-TOWN

Looks like the Connellys have been plunged into scandal yet again—Grant Connelly's former lover, Ms. Angie Donahue, has been arrested! Sources report that Ms. Donahue, the mother of Grant's illegitimate son, Seth Connelly, is the niece of Chicago's most influential mob boss, Jimmy Kelly. Police investigations leading up to her arrest indicate that the Kellys may be behind the recent spate of troubles that have plagued the prestigious Connelly family these last few months.

And how is Seth Connelly, a well-respected attorney in the Windy City, taking this news? It seems that Seth has taken an undetermined leave of absence from his law practice...and from Chicago. Sources close to the thirty-two-year-old bachelor say he has been devastated by his mother's revelation, but won't reveal his location.

The Connelly troubles don't end there. Following police questioning, Grant's longtime assistant, Charlotte Masters, has also gone missing—and rumor has it that her life may be in danger. And she's not the only one. Police report that hotshot P.I. Tom Reynolds, hired to protect the family, has turned up dead, the apparent victim of foul play.

In the wake of these latest disclosures, we expect local sympathies to be with Seth, a reserved lone wolf who never became a true bachelor-about-town like so many of the Connelly sons. Chicago awaits his return!

Dear Reader,

This season of harvest brings a cornucopia of six new passionate, powerful and provocative love stories from Silhouette Desire for your enjoyment.

Don't miss our current MAN OF THE MONTH title, Cindy Gerard's *Taming the Outlaw,* a reunion romance featuring a cowboy dealing with the unexpected consequences of a hometown summer of passion. And of course you'll want to read Katherine Garbera's *Cinderella's Convenient Husband,* the tenth absorbing title in Silhouette Desire's DYNASTIES: THE CONNELLYS continuity series.

A Navy SEAL is on a mission to win the love of the woman he left behind, in *The SEAL's Surprise Baby* by Amy J. Fetzer, while a TV anchorwoman gets up close and personal with a high-ranking soldier in *The Royal Treatment* by Maureen Child. This is the latest title in the exciting Silhouette crossline series CROWN AND GLORY.

Opposites attract when a sexy hunk and a matchmaker share digs in *Hearts Are Wild* by Laura Wright. And in *Secrets, Lies and...Passion* by Linda Conrad, a single mom is drawn into a web of desire and danger by the lover who jilted her at the altar years before...or did he?

Experience all six of these sensuous romances from Silhouette Desire this month, and guarantee that your Halloween will be all treat, no trick.

Enjoy!

Joan Marlow Golan

Joan Marlow Golan
Senior Editor, Silhouette Desire

Cinderella's Convenient Husband

KATHERINE GARBERA

Published by Silhouette Books
America's Publisher of Contemporary Romance

Special thanks and acknowledgment are given to Katherine Garbera for her contribution to the DYNASTIES: THE CONNELYS series.

For Maureen Walters, who is encouraging while at the same time realistic. Thanks for your support.

SILHOUETTE BOOKS

ISBN 0-373-76466-9

CINDERELLA'S CONVENIENT HUSBAND

This edition published by arrangement with Harlequin Books S.A.

Visit Silhouette at www.eHarlequin.com

Printed in U.S.A.

Books by Katherine Garbera

Silhouette Desire

The Bachelor Next Door #1104
Miranda's Outlaw #1169
Her Baby's Father #1289
Overnight Cinderella #1348
Baby at His Door #1367
Some Kind of Incredible #1395
The Tycoon's Temptation #1414
The Tycoon's Lady #1464
Cinderella's Convenient Husband #1466

KATHERINE GARBERA

loves a happy ending, so writing romance came naturally to her. She is a native Floridian who was recently transplanted to the Chicago area. "Living in a place where there are seasons is strange," says Garbera. Her stories are known for their lush character detail and sensuality. She is happily married to the man she met in Fantasyland and has two children. She is an active member of Romance Writers of America, Novelists Inc. and The Authors' Guild. Visit her home page on the Web at www.katherinegarbera.com.

MEET THE CONNELLYS

Meet the Connellys of Chicago—
wealthy, powerful and rocked by scandal,
betrayal...and passion!

Who's Who in
CINDERELLA'S CONVENIENT HUSBAND

Seth Connelly—Deceived and betrayed by his heritage once again, he runs away, back to his cowboy roots, hoping to find himself, to heal....

Lynn McCoy—She knows what it's like to be betrayed by someone you love—and now she, too, is paying the price.

Angie Donahue—Seth's mother; she allowed his father, Grant Connelly, to raise him, but the havoc she wreaks finds her son wherever he hides....

One

"What can I get for you?" asked the blond waitress.

Seth Connelly looked straight into eyes he'd never forgotten. They were the deep purple of crushed African violets. Lynn McCoy had been a troublemaking brat for the first five years of their acquaintance then she'd blossomed into a beautiful young woman. One who tempted him to forget that her older brother was closer to him than his own.

"Hello, Lynn," he said. Somehow when he'd thought of those he might see in Sagebrush, Montana, he'd forgotten about Lynn and that one awkward kiss they'd shared the night of her sixteenth birthday.

He'd never returned to the ranch again, aware that he'd crossed a line that shouldn't have been crossed.

Aware that he'd taken a step that would alienate him from Matt. Aware that it was time to stop running and return home to Chicago.

But his birth mother's betrayal had made Chicago into a tense place, and he'd hit the road hoping to find some semblance of the man he'd become. Because as he'd fallen once again for Angie Donahue's lies and manipulation, he'd realized that he didn't know himself anymore.

He hoped Lynn didn't remember the embrace—it was so long ago. But life had taught him that if she did, more than likely it haunted her. That one brief brush of lips still plagued his dreams on restless nights, because she had tasted innocent and he never had been.

Her eyes widened in recognition and she smiled at him. There was weariness on her face, and an instinctual part of him recognized that expression for what it was. She was running from something as well.

Not your business, old man.

"Hi, Seth. What brings you to our little corner of the world?"

He was a successful lawyer from a wealthy family so he knew all about people who complained when they had plenty, and he wouldn't be one of those. He couldn't tell her that he'd come here searching for something that he'd found in his youth. Something he couldn't really explain to anyone. It had been a feeling, really, maybe something more but not definable.

"I'm hoping for a cup of coffee and a steak."

"You've come to the right place. But I should tell you it's probably not as fancy as you'd get in Chicago."

"That's okay. The atmosphere's better here."

"Really? I'd have thought all those sophisticated people would win hands down."

"Nothing beats the mountains in Montana." Even though night had fallen, the view from the diner was one he'd never forgotten.

"You can say that again."

Their eyes met and held in a moment of pure appreciation for what nature had so splendidly given this area of the country.

"What kind of dressing do you want on your salad?"

He told her and she walked away. The quiet conversation that buzzed around him reminded him why he liked Sagebrush. Here in this small town he wasn't the illegitimate son of a Mafia princess and Chicago's most revered citizen. Here he was that wild boy who'd had his ear pierced and wore a leather jacket even in the heat of summer. Here he was a man without a family—and Seth needed that.

Here he was a friend of the McCoys and treated as such. That warm feeling was why he'd returned in late fall when winter beckoned around the corner.

Lynn brought his coffee and salad and then hurried away to take care of the rest of her tables. Another waiter brought his steak, which was perfectly cooked.

The meal was one of the best he'd had in a long

time, simple food prepared for taste instead of presentation. Seth knew he'd made the right decision. The tension that had been dogging him receded. It didn't disappear completely but ebbed enough for him to relax his shoulders.

Lynn looked tired, he thought.

And not unlike his half-sister Tara had looked when she'd been trying to have her missing husband Michael declared legally dead. What kind of problems hung on her shoulders? Why wasn't Matt here to relieve that burden for her? He knew that Matt McCoy and he shared more than friendship but also an overwhelming urge to protect those dear to them.

What was Matt thinking to let his sister work in a diner when there wasn't any reason for it? The McCoy spread was the biggest and most profitable in the area. Seth knew this not only from his youth but also from his yearly treks to meet Matt for vacations. They always discussed the ranch. But never Lynn.

She stopped by to refill his coffee cup. "Can you join me for a minute?"

"Just real quick."

"You're a hard worker, Lynn."

"Thank you," she said tentatively.

"Why the hesitation?"

"The last time you complimented me I found myself soaking wet on a cold evening."

"Hey, you're safe for now. I've grown into a boring old lawyer," he said.

"Not boring or old. Lawyer?"

"Okay, get it out of your system," he said, knowing few people could resist the urge to lob a few lawyer jokes when they actually met one.

"What?" she asked, all innocence. She looked breathtakingly lovely in the dim light of the diner.

"You've got to have a joke about lawyers."

"Not me. Besides, I have nothing but respect for you," she said.

"Yeah, right. If memory serves, the last prank you played on me involved stealing my clothes and leaving me naked at the swimming hole."

"I left your hat, didn't I?"

It had been uncomfortable to be outsmarted by a girl a few years younger than he was. Because at home no one got the jump on Seth Connelly. He still felt a little embarrassed when he recalled the number of times she'd gotten the better of him. "I think we're square."

"Yeah, I think so. Are you here to see Matt?"

"Yes."

"He's not home."

"I thought his tour ended last month."

"It did but he was on an assignment that he felt needed him and reupped."

Damn. He wasn't going to be able to stay at the McCoy Ranch if Matt wasn't there. He'd counted on the wide-open spaces, the cattle lowing in the distance and the fragrance of jasmine to lull him to sleep.

"I'm surprised you didn't call first."

"I didn't know I was coming until I got here."

She nodded. "I've got to get back to work. You take care, Seth Connelly."

She walked away and this time he watched and wanted. She was exactly as he remembered from that late-summer night. Sweet and funny but tempered with the experiences life had used to test her. And he knew that it was probably for the best that Matt wasn't here and Seth would be moving on...again.

Lynn McCoy let the smile drop from her face the minute she entered the kitchen. She'd been worried that maybe Matt had sent him. But it seemed he was only looking for Matt, not trying to find out what kind of trouble she was in. Trouble was about the only thing she had right now.

And it looked as if another helping was on the way. Childhood crushes were supposed to end well before thirty. Lynn knew this in her rational mind but her heart beat a little bit faster as she thought about Seth Connelly. He hardly resembled the rough loner who'd first visited her family's ranch the summer she was eleven.

Now he had the kind of quiet self-assurance he'd lacked as a youth. Though his gray eyes were stormy like the north Atlantic, his body language said there was nothing he couldn't handle.

He'd looked surprised to see her at the diner. She knew he had to be. After all, the prosperous McCoy ranch had never failed to support the generations.

What had brought him to Montana in October?

There wasn't much in the way of tourism in Sagebrush. Besides, she knew he was involved in his family's business and wondered if he was having family problems again.

Part of what had initially drawn her to Seth had been that he was so alone. Though she knew she could never really trust him, her brother considered Seth closer than a blood relation.

Her first impulse had been to settle into the booth with him and spend the evening catching up on the past, but she knew that she fell in love too easily and she'd learned that lesson the hard way. She felt almost proud of the way she resisted that urge.

She waved good-night to the cook and left before she gave in and returned to the corner booth where Seth sat. Keep walking, Lynn. The night air bit into her clothes and she shivered in her leather coat. It had been her grandfather's and would keep her warm once she buttoned it.

The employee parking area was well lit, and Lynn approached her truck with no trepidation. But the stenciling on the side gave her pause. The McCoy Ranch—Home Of The Best Beef In Montana.

For how much longer? She had barely one hundred head left because that was all she could work on her own and still make ends meet. Tears burned the back of her eyes at her own stupidity. Trusting too easily had been her biggest weakness. Though she'd never be able to look at the world with a truly cynical eye, a part of her had been forever changed when Ronnie had taken her money and left her.

The highway ran behind the fence and she listened to the cars flying past. She'd never understood the obsession everyone had with getting out of Sagebrush. She'd loved her hometown and had never ventured farther than the airport in Billings to pick up friends.

Suddenly her entire world was in danger of falling apart and she was at the end of the line. She'd tried everything she could. She'd sold all the horses except for Thor, her gelding, leased part of the grazing pasture, boarded horses for the folks in town and taken this job. But there still was more debt than she could cover.

What was she going to do? Her plan, which had seemed so brilliant in the middle of the night, seemed a little weak today. She'd worked double shifts at the diner, and as she waited on tables, her mind had puzzled over the options.

There seemed damn few. Then the past had to walk in the front door like the precursor to a bad storm and look at her as if she was…what? A woman. It had been a long time since any man had looked at her like that. Ronnie had taken more with him than she'd realized. He'd taken part of her femininity with him, leaving her vulnerable and unsure in the one area she'd always been confident.

"Lynn?" Seth's voice brushed over her like a warm wind, but she knew better than to believe what it promised. A man's silky voice at night had never brought her anything but pain.

Damn. Instead of a clean getaway, now she was going to have to face him again. She pivoted toward him. He was cast half in shadows by the lamplight. His features were sharp and bold and for a minute he looked more comfortable than she'd ever seen him.

That disturbed her, but she shook it off. She needed to get home and get a good night's sleep so she'd be prepared for her meeting tomorrow.

"Yes, Seth?"

"Why are you working here?"

"I like the change of pace."

She'd never been able to look anyone in the eye while she lied to him. And it had gotten her into hot water more than once.

"You look tired," he said.

She felt the fatigue as if for the first time. She glanced up and met his gaze. He compelled her to tell him the truth and she did. Just a little bit, a sop for her conscience. "I am."

"Why are you really working here?"

"I don't know. The people, I guess."

"Really?"

"Yes, it's too quiet at the ranch." That was the truth. With the hands gone and the big old house to herself, she needed some conversation to distract her.

"If you ever need anything, Lynn, let me know. I owe your family." She'd never seen him so earnest before. She'd seen him tough and ready to take on three older boys in a fight. She'd seen him eager to learn how to rope and brand cattle. She'd seen him with his dreams in his eyes as he'd looked at the night sky and told Matt about the solar system.

"You don't owe us anything. You worked those summers you spent here." And he'd given her brother someone to imitate. Someone to bond with and look up to. Especially after Daddy had died. She thought maybe the McCoys owed Seth more than he'd ever know.

A red tinge colored his neck. "Well, I tried to do my part."

She realized then that Seth wasn't all that comfortable with praise, and it made him seem a little more human. "I've got to go."

"Will you give Matt this note when he comes home?" he asked, holding out a sheet of legal paper that had been folded neatly into thirds. Matt's name was printed in large block letters. There was nothing timid about Seth, she thought.

"Sure," she said, trying to convince herself that whatever she'd felt for Seth Connelly had died a long time ago. But somehow her hormones didn't get that message. Her skin tingled when their fingers brushed. Her breath seemed harder to come by and her heart beat a bit faster. Chills spread up her arm. Her nipples tightened and her breasts felt heavy. For some reason her feet seemed planted to the ground.

She recognized the symptoms. *Lust.* Not now, she thought. Not again. The last time she'd followed her impulses around Seth she'd ended up brokenhearted. She'd learned too much and come too far from that sixteen-year-old girl to behave that way again. Or at least as a thirty year old she'd like to hope she did.

"I'll stick it in the next letter I mail him," she said.

"Thank you."

She tugged her hand out from under his. "You're welcome."

She didn't like the way he made her feel. Didn't like that for the first time since Ronnie had taken her money and her heart, she was interested in a man. Especially didn't like that the man was Seth.

Resolutely, she marched toward her truck and unlocked the door.

"Uh, Lynn?" When she turned to look at him, his eyes held the maturity of age and she knew that whatever she remembered of him she'd always liked him. Which was dangerous to her. Because he looked as if he needed a shoulder to cry on.

"Yes?"

He rubbed the bridge of his nose and then stepped closer to her. "It occurs to me that I owe you an apology."

Oh, God. "I can't imagine why."

He moved another step closer. So close she could smell the coffee he'd drunk with dinner. "For that kiss I stole when you were sixteen."

She didn't want to have this conversation with Seth now. *Never* sounded like a good time to chat about it.

"You didn't steal it."

"I felt like I did after I walked away without a word."

"Hey, I'm a mature woman now. I barely remember an embrace that long ago."

"Really?"

No, but she'd rather give away the ranch than admit it. She shrugged.

"It haunts me," he said simply. He started to walk away, his shoulders set and his stride bold.

His words cut through the protective layers she'd wrapped around herself. "Seth?"

He stopped, glancing over his shoulder at her. A light snow began to fall and it dusted his head and black trench coat.

"I..."

He nodded. She wasn't sure he understood what she'd been trying to say.

"Me too," she said finally and opened the door to her truck. She climbed in quickly and drove away, watching Seth standing there in the lightly falling snow.

For the first time in months she didn't dream about the ranch or the diner. Instead, a pair of silver eyes plagued her dreams.

Two

It was well after midnight when Seth gave up trying to find a motel and turned down the familiar road that led to the McCoy ranch. He consoled himself with the thought that he could sleep in the bunkhouse with the ranch hands but he knew Lynn's bed was where he really wanted to spend the night. A light flickered over the porch as the house came into view. A sole pickup was parked next to the kitchen entrance.

He pulled his Jag to a stop and went to the bunkhouse. It was deserted and locked up tight. Questions formed quicker than he could answer them. But he was tired and would seek those answers in the morning.

It was cold outside and he doubted he'd survive the

night if he slept in the car. His options were limited. He'd have to disturb Lynn.

Only fair, his raging hormones agreed, since she'd been disturbing him all evening.

In the old days a spare key had been kept under the potted planter on the front porch. He was glad to see at least that hadn't changed. He unlocked the door, replacing the key before he entered quietly. That was the one good thing to be said for a misspent youth; he knew how to move so silently that no one could hear him.

He turned left off the entryway toward the living room. As he made his way to the couch, he slammed into an ottoman that hadn't been there in his memory and cursed under his breath. His shins ached and he heard footsteps upstairs.

"Matt, is that you?" Lynn's voice was sleepy and husky.

Awareness tingled down his spine and stirred the flesh between his legs. He walked to the foyer and flipped on the hallway light. "No, it's Seth."

She descended the stairs before taking time to get a robe. The silk long johns she wore did little to mask her body, instead it seemed to frame it in a way meant to tease a man. But her clothes, imprinted with cartoon characters, clearly weren't articles of seduction. She should have looked sweet and innocent instead of seductive. "Seth, what are you doing in my house?"

"There's no place to stay in town."

She stopped a few feet from him. He hadn't realized earlier how much taller than she he was. She barely cleared his breastbone. His libido supplied him with the image of the two of them naked in a bed where she'd fit very comfortably into his arms.

She's my best friend's little sister, he reminded himself.

"Where are you headed?" she asked.

Straight to hell, he thought. He cleared his throat. "This is my destination."

"Oh."

"I thought I'd bunk with the men," he said so that she wouldn't suspect that he wanted her.

"No, you can't. You'd better stay up here." She wouldn't look him in the eye, and he knew it was because she was planning on making up some story about where the cowpokes were who used to live there.

"I've been to the bunkhouse, Lynn. What happened?"

"Oh, we don't have such a great need for overnight staff anymore." Her hair fell to the middle of her back in tousled waves and the light reflected in it. He'd always loved her hair. Even as a tomboy teenager she'd had miles of hair. After she turned sixteen it had played into more than one of his fantasies while he'd slept under this roof.

"Why not?" he asked, trying to focus on anything but her body.

She sighed. "It's the middle of the night and you must be tired."

Seth knew the gentlemanly thing to do would be to get in his car and drive back down the highway until he found a place to stay, but he was tired.

"Can I stay here tonight? I'll head back to Chicago in the morning." He'd been turned out of better places and for less reason than Lynn had.

She touched his arm, and though he knew it was impossible, he seemed to feel her heat through the layers of his jacket and shirt. "Of course you can. I didn't mean you should leave."

"Thank you. I'll grab my overnight bag and bunk down here," he said. She'd tilted her head back to look him in the eye now that they were standing so close, and he realized she had a long, graceful neck. Her skin looked as pale as the moonbeams, and he wondered if it would taste as sweet as it looked.

"Do you really want to sleep on the sofa?"

"No. But I don't want to disturb you."

"You won't. I didn't even hear you enter the house."

"I can be very quiet."

"And then really noisy. What happened?"

"The ottoman."

She chuckled. "Are you okay? I've hit that thing a time or two myself."

The piece was old and heavy, made of solid oak with a pretty, embroidered covering that he knew Mrs. McCoy had made during her first year of marriage. It was a tradition in the McCoy family that the newlyweds made a piece of furniture for their new life together.

"Go get your bag. You can sleep in Matt's room. I'll change the sheets for you."

"Thanks, Lynn."

"No problem, Seth."

The way she said his name made him wonder if she wasn't remembering what it had been like to kiss him. And though he knew that would be a big mistake, it was all he could think of as he retrieved his overnight bag from the car. Think of her as your own sister, he cautioned himself. He tried to imagine one of his half sisters in those long johns waiting upstairs for him. But as he entered the house and climbed the stairs, he knew it wasn't Alexandra, Tara or Maggie up there.

Even an image of Matt's glowering face couldn't keep his blood from flowing heavier or his loins from tightening. The only one who could do that was he. And the one thing Seth had always been able to do was keep his cool and his control. Why, then, did it feel as if he was barely hanging on?

Lynn turned off the shower at nine the next morning. She'd been up since dawn feeding Thor and the other horses that she boarded for the townsfolk. She'd slept better last night than she'd expected to. The security of knowing she wasn't alone on the ranch should have been enough to ensure she didn't spend the night twisting and turning in her bed. But Seth's icy gaze and warm touch had haunted her dreams.

She'd hurried out of bed and refused to dwell on those thoughts. Seth was nothing more to her than an old family friend, and she didn't have too many of them left. Most had died or moved on, leaving her alone for almost five years. Longer than she'd ever expected. Perhaps that loneliness was why she was so willing to latch on to Seth.

She had an appointment at the bank this morning and needed to get dressed. Her closet was a fashion nightmare, dominated by faded jeans and western shirts. In the back, in a plastic dry-cleaning bag, was her one suit, some designer label that she'd bought to wear to her mother's funeral.

She dressed in it quickly but with care. If she had a chance of persuading Mr. Cochran at the bank to extend the loan, she needed to exude success. But how did success look? Seth would know, she thought.

It was too bad she couldn't tell him the truth, because she could use his advice. He knew about making money. Heck, he came from one of the wealthiest families in Chicago. But he'd tell Matt and she wasn't going to ask her big brother to bail her out of another mess.

She twisted her long hair into a chignon and applied the light makeup that she wore to church. The suit was cut with classic lines that flattered her lean frame. For a minute she glimpsed who she might have been if her family had lived in a city instead of this small rural town.

She didn't hear any signs of life from Matt's room as she walked down the stairs. Maybe she could sneak out before Seth woke. He'd be gone when she returned and she wouldn't have to see him again.

The smell of coffee warned her that her luck was running par. She entered the kitchen and poured herself a cup of coffee. At the breakfast table Seth had set up a laptop computer attached to her phone jack.

He made a few keystrokes on the computer and then turned to smile at her. For a minute she forgot why she thought she couldn't trust him.

"Good morning." His voice was low and husky, masculine in the early morning. She wasn't used to a man's voice and it startled her. Seth had obviously taken a shower before coming downstairs and was dressed again in casual elegance.

"Morning," she said, gulping her coffee and scalding her tongue. She hated it when she did that. Damn, if she was this rattled on her home turf, how was she going to handle the bank?

"Sleep well?" he asked, eyeing her. She wondered if she'd smudged her lipstick on her teeth. Surreptitiously she rubbed her tongue over her front teeth.

"Yes." She sat down across from him.

"Good, because I have some questions."

"About?" Not now, she thought.

"The ranch, Lynn. What the hell happened?"

She knew he'd ask. Anyone with eyes would wonder the same thing. But her answers were hard to come by. She was a proud woman—always had been—and telling this smart, handsome man that she'd fallen for a con was not in the game plan.

"Times are tough. NAFTA didn't do ranchers a favor."

"Most of the ranches aren't this bad."

She glanced over his shoulder at the wallpaper that had once been a bright spring floral print but had faded with time. She had a moment's fear that she was glimpsing the future. That someday she'd be as old and faded as the wallpaper and have seen just as little of life.

Carefully she considered her words. "True, but most of them aren't run by one person."

"The McCoy ranch never has been in the past."

"Well, it is now."

"Lynn, unless you want me to place an emergency call to your brother, you better start talking."

"Why?" she demanded. Seth had been away for a long time, and though she knew he had fond memories of the summers he'd spent here, they couldn't be reason enough for him to probe into ranch matters.

"What?" he asked.

"You heard me. Why do you care what's happened?"

He sighed and rubbed the bridge of his nose with his thumb and forefinger. He looked stressed. She wondered if this questioning wasn't his way of hiding from whatever had driven him from Chicago. No matter what he'd said the night before she didn't believe he just felt like visiting her brother on an impulse.

"This ranch is important to me." Seth's sincerity had never been more apparent.

"Then why haven't you been back for fourteen years?"

"It's not my ancestral home."

"I'm doing my best to save it."

"What do you think Matt will say when he sees this place?"

"It won't look like this when he comes home."

"Really?"

"Yes, I have big plans."

"Tell me what's going on."

"I can't."

"Why not?"

"Because you won't understand."

"Trust me, Lynn. I'm on your side."

"The last time I trusted you, you kissed me and walked away."

"Is that what this is all about?"

"Of course not. I'm just saying your track record isn't the best."

"And yours is?"

"I didn't walk away."

"You didn't come after me either."

"I don't want to have this conversation. I'm due at the bank at ten and I don't want to be late."

"Just tell me what's going on. Is it money? Maybe I can help."

"Why are you here, Seth?"

He was silent.

"That's right," she said with a nod. "You have your own secrets and I have mine. Let's keep them that way."

"Your family meant a lot to me."

"I know. But it's better this way. Besides, you're leaving today."

"I could still help you."

"No, you can't. But I'll make a note that you tried."

Lynn walked away from him wishing she felt a little more confident. Wishing for a miracle she knew she had faint hope of getting. Wishing that Seth wasn't leaving today.

"Lynn, wait. I'll drive you into town."

She'd gathered her purse and a sheaf of documents. This was a Lynn he'd never seen before. He'd be lying if he said she didn't attract him. She wasn't the rough-and-ready ranch girl that he didn't know how to handle. For the moment she was a city woman, like every other woman in his life.

She glanced over her shoulder at him, her eyes hidden by a pair of dark glasses. Mystery surrounded her, and Seth wanted to investigate the changes. Would the real Lynn McCoy please stand up?

"I'd rather take myself."

Of course you would, Ms. Independent. She reminded him of his stepmother and sisters. They'd take any challenge but they'd do it in their own unique ways. And he knew he had to respect Lynn's way of doing things even if it wasn't his own.

Reality intruded. She'd said she was going to the bank. More than likely that meant she needed money and the only way she was going to get it was to look as if she didn't need it. The Jag was a showy car, pricey and elegant; it spoke volumes for whoever drove it without him having to say a word. It had netted him invitations to the nicest residences in Chicago, even though he knew many of those old-money folks looked down on him because of his dubious parentage.

"The banker will be more likely to listen to whatever you have to say if you arrive in the Jag."

"Okay, but I drive." The haughty look she'd conjured up made him want to kiss her. She seemed untouchable in her upswept hairdo and her fancy suit. He wanted to rumple her up and find the girl who'd let him sleep in her home last night. To find the girl with hair hanging down her back wearing silky long johns.

Though Lynn's suit made her look more like the other women he knew, he realized that he wanted her to be different. The thought floored him. Maybe he had an ulterior motive for wanting to help?

But he knew more than lust motivated him. There was a soft spot in his soul for the McCoys.

"No one drives my Jag." He spoke from the gut.

The car was as important to him as his laptop or his Swiss timepiece. He wasn't going to chance it.

"Now where's the trust?" she asked softly. Her words cut right through the superficiality of what he'd been thinking.

He did feel a bit like a child on Christmas morning who'd been asked to share his new toy. "Who's talking about trust? This car is a finely tuned machine and you're used to driving that tank over there."

"Is it the car you're worried about or your tough-guy image?"

He remained unfazed. "Whatever the reason, the result is the same. I'm driving."

Deliberately he walked to the passenger side of the car to open the door for her. "What a gentleman you are, Seth Connelly. Too bad I know the real you."

Though he knew Lynn had meant her remarks as something else entirely, she'd struck a nerve. "I think the door's unlocked."

She didn't know the real Seth—no one did. And he'd made it his life's mission to make sure that the situation stayed that way. He didn't like Lynn's innuendo that he was less than civilized. But maybe there was a kernel of truth in her words. Underneath his civilized veneer beat the heart of a warrior, not a Prince Charming.

He'd never been anyone's white knight but he was the guy they'd turned to in a fight, knowing he'd never lose. That had been true at twelve when he'd come to the Connellys and it was true now in the courtroom where he won every battle he took up.

Whether Lynn liked it or not, he was in her corner. The debt he owed the McCoy family was too big for him to not step up to the plate now.

Five years of military school and six years of college had ensured that he could converse within any circle and not embarrass his family. Lessons from his stepmom, Emma Connelly, on deportment and manners had made sure he was every inch the gentleman.

''Are you going to check the door?'' she asked.

Seth realized he'd been standing next to the car. He should just turn around, lock the door and drive her to town. He should pretend that her words hadn't ripped away a scab he'd never known was there. He should not lean down so that her face was only inches from his and her sweet breath brushed across his cheek.

''I don't think anyone knows the real Seth.''

She cupped his jaw in her hand and Seth was humbled by the touch even as it started a series of fires throughout his body and brought the hardness to his loins that had made sleep uncomfortable all night.

''I do.''

''Then who is he, Lynn?''

''He's a man who's strong and loyal. A man willing to go to any lengths for those he cares for, even putting up with the tantrums of his best friend's younger sister.''

"You weren't throwing a tantrum. You were right. I don't like to share my things."

"That's because you've never been sure they were really yours." Her insight was a smooth balm over his aching wounds, and he stood before he did something stupid like kiss her.

He closed the door firmly and went to the house to make sure it was secured. As he walked back to the car, he tried to tell himself he'd resisted Lynn because she was Matt's sister. Tried to tell himself it was because she was in trouble and needed his help. But deep inside he knew the real reason—she saw too much of who he really was.

Three

Lynn held her breath until Seth drove off of her property, leaving behind the visual reminder of her mistake. She'd trusted her heart to a smooth-talking man from New York City who'd promised to give her the world and share her life. And then convinced her to mortgage the ranch and put the money into a short-term, high-yield fund.

The only thing Ronnie had forgotten to mention was that he'd be the only one getting rich from her money. He disappeared with her cash exactly eighteen months ago.

Seth pulled the Jag to a stop on the shoulder of the road. Her first thought was they'd run out of gas. But she soon realized that Seth had given in only to get his own way.

"We're not going any farther until you tell me what's going on."

Tears burned the back of her eyes. He'd driven far enough that she couldn't walk back to the ranch and still make her appointment at the bank. Time was running out. She heard the beating of the countdown clock in her mind and she could scarcely breathe as she stared at the long, empty road ahead of her.

She felt cornered and betrayed by someone who'd lulled her into feeling safe. The sensation was much the same as the one she'd experienced when she'd realized Ronnie was never coming back. She knew of only one way out of this situation. Actually, two—fighting or telling the truth.

Seth Connelly might wear the trappings of civilization, might have spent the last twenty years with a silver spoon in his mouth, but underneath the exterior beat the heart of a street warrior who'd seen the seamier side of life. She knew he'd come from the mean streets of one of Chicago's most dangerous neighborhoods before his mom left him with the Connellys.

Military school had honed that rebellious boy into a controlled man who knew how to manipulate circumstances for his own good. And though she knew in her heart that he wasn't acting out of malice, her pride chafed at having been fooled once again by a man.

Truth was really the only option she had left. But she had to ensure some provisos before telling him anything. Matt mustn't be put into jeopardy because she'd listened to her heart instead of her head.

"I want you to promise me you won't call Matt or interfere."

Rubbing his jaw, Seth shook his head. "I can't make any promises until I hear the circumstances." For the first time, she understood how different their personalities were.

She would have agreed to the stipulation without thinking the entire situation through. But Seth was cautious. Maybe he could offer her some other ideas than the one she'd come up with—selling off part of her ranch.

She took a deep breath and looked out the window at the barren landscape. Montana was preparing for winter. The deep freeze within which she'd surrounded herself began to thaw just a little as she talked about the situation for the first time with someone other than a loan officer.

"The ranch is being foreclosed on in nine days."

Resting one arm behind her on the seat and the other on the dash, he leaned toward Lynn. She felt his presence everywhere; it was totally nonthreatening, yet at the same time arousing. He smelled crisp and clean with a faint spicy aroma. He moved the hand to her shoulder, urging her to look at him.

He's your brother's best friend, she reminded herself.

She met his gaze. It was hot and heavy, filled with questions and something more. Her skin tingled, and she forgot that he'd maneuvered her to this place where she was acting on his will. Forgot that he was her brother's friend and he'd owe his loyalty to Matt. Forgot that the last time she'd thrown caution to the wind for a man she'd ended up in this situation.

Snap out of it, girl. She leaned away from him, pressing her back against the cold glass of the window. Everything would be easier if he wasn't attracted to her. When she mixed with men, things ended in disaster.

"How did that happen?" he asked, his tone so matter-of-fact that she thought he might be a researcher following clues to a new discovery.

I don't know, she thought. You come close to me, and my mind shuts down. Then she realized he'd meant the foreclosure.

"There was this guy, Ronnie. He gave a seminar on investing and I took his advice. The deal went south, and I was left with a mortgaged ranch."

"Things are never that simple. I need more details."

No way, she thought. She wasn't going to tell Seth Connelly that she'd fallen for blue eyes, blond hair and an all-American smile. That she'd mortgaged her property so that Ronnie would stay with her instead of moving on to Los Angeles and the promise of bigger investors. That she'd given her soul to a man without one.

"You mortgaged the land to get the capital to invest?"

She nodded.

"Where did he invest your money?"

"Supposedly on Wall Street."

"Supposedly?"

"It seems I fell victim to a con man."

He cursed.

"I know it sounds unbelievable but it didn't at the time."

"It never does. What have you told Matt?"

"Nothing. His job is very risky. I don't want him thinking about me and the ranch instead of his assignment. I can't bury another member of my family, Seth."

"I know," he said, caressing her jaw.

Silence fell and they both stared at each other.

"What's the plan?" Seth asked.

"I've been working double shifts at the diner and have been boarding horses for the folks who live in town. I've got about five thousand I can give the bank today. I'm hoping that will be enough to buy me some time."

"What are you going to do with the time?"

"Find a buyer for the outer land. I hate to give up even an acre of the property, but I can't lose the house."

The thought of anyone other than the McCoys owning the land seemed like sacrilege to him. But at the same time her dilemma was his way out of what he owed her family. It was ironic that he'd visited the ranch as a boy with no money and he'd returned a wealthy man. The solution seemed obvious to Seth.

"I'll pay off your loan and you can pay me back."

She smiled at him, and it was the saddest expression he'd ever seen. If he'd had a heart, he thought it would have broken. Her deep violet eyes were wide and watery as she tried to keep from crying.

"Seth, that's so sweet. But I...no."

Lynn shouldn't look like this, he thought. She should be riding her horse across the same land she'd ridden as a child. Never should anyone else own an acre of land that had been the McCoys since pioneers had first settled in the West.

"Lynn, be reasonable." If she took the money, he could leave and not be tormented by images of the two of them making love in her bed. Or, he thought, leaning closer to her in the front of his car, if he put the seat back, she'd fit nicely in his lap.

She's your best friend's little sister, he reminded himself. But his body didn't care about that.

"Reason has nothing to do with this. I can't take your money. If Matt were here, he'd do the same thing."

Seth struggled to remember that he wanted her to take the money so he could go. Returning to Chicago wasn't what he wanted right now, but it seemed safer than staying in Montana and tempting himself with a woman he knew was off limits.

"Matt would pay the loan off himself or take my money."

She considered the idea for all of a second. ''It's not Matt's debt to pay nor yours. Don't suggest it again.''

''The next time a woman tells me how hardheaded men are, I'm going to direct her to you.'' Her jaw clenched and she didn't look as if she was going to cry anymore. Slug him maybe, but not break down.

''I'm not stubborn just—''

''Proud,'' he said. He couldn't blame her. If he were in her shoes, he'd do whatever he had to—on his own. He wasn't a team player and he knew it. He was more the alpha wolf leading his pack, and now he wanted to protect one of his own. Because whether Lynn knew it or not, she was definitely his.

Where had that come from? He didn't know, but it made an odd sort of sense. Taking care of Lynn the way her family had taken care of him in those summers long ago would fill something in him that had been empty too long.

''I believe in paying my own way,'' she said. ''I made this mess and I'll be the one to clean it up.''

She was so close he could smell the sweetness of her perfume and the underlying scent of woman. He closed his eyes. It's about money, man. Keep your mind there.

''How about if I make you a loan and you can make payments to me?''

''Seth, be serious. You're never going to take my family's land.''

She was right. He'd deed the land back to her as

soon as the paperwork was finalized. But he was in a position to give a gift that huge if he wanted to. And he wanted to. He thought it might be more of a need because he was so hard right now, if they didn't compromise on the bank soon he was going to try putting his seat back and pulling her across his thighs. And that was something he shouldn't do.

He'd tried one time to bridge the gap between them and he'd ended up leaving Montana and hurting Lynn in the process. He wouldn't hurt her again.

"What do you suggest?"

She closed her eyes and bowed her head, looking defeated. That was the one way he'd never wanted to see this proud woman. She should be standing tall.

"Going to the bank and talking to Cochran. Which, by the way, we should be doing now."

"I'm not driving anywhere until we find a solution that has at least a fifty-fifty shot of working."

He'd never met a woman who didn't look out for herself first, to the exclusion of anyone else. Lynn was totally different from his mother. A woman who'd used his birth to milk his father's family for more than money. But there was a part of him that believed she'd do the thing that would keep her in comfort.

"I guess this is stalemate."

"I'm not going to stop at anything short of complete surrender."

"Why?" she asked, glancing up at him.

"This place was my saving grace, Lynn, and I won't let anyone, even you, throw it away."

"I can't take money from my brother's best friend."

"Who can you take money from?"

"Matt."

"It seems we're back to the beginning."

"Let's go into town and let me meet with Cochran. He might agree to my plan. Or perhaps he'll agree to take the land and leave me the house."

"I don't want your land in anyone's hands other than yours."

"I'm always going to remember how noble you were about this, Seth."

"I've never been noble but I do know right from wrong, and what you're proposing doesn't feel right."

"It's the only way."

He didn't say another word, just turned forward and started the car. He drove into town, his mind swimming with possibilities. He'd let Lynn try to work her deal with the bank, and if that didn't work, he'd arrange for one of the banks that he used in Chicago to buy the loan. He knew there was a way to manipulate the banks and the system for it to seem as if Lynn were still making payments to the institution, when in reality she'd be making payments to him.

Part of him chafed at the thought of deceiving this woman to whom pride meant so much, but another part realized that there were times when the situation called for desperate measures. As the thought entered his head, he wondered if his mother had ever justified using him by just the same thought.

* * *

Lynn left the bank with a heavy heart and anger pulsing through her veins. She'd never met a person she couldn't out-stubborn until this morning. Cochran wanted her land—but he wanted all of it and he wanted her out of the house in less than ten days.

Seth leaned casually against the hood of his car. Give him a cigarette and a leather jacket and he'd look the same as he had fourteen years ago. Her heart pounded a little faster at the sight of him, but she knew that nothing could come of it. Men were bad news for her.

"What did he say?" Seth asked, straightening as she approached.

She tried to utter the words, but her throat closed and she had to wrinkle her nose to keep the tears from falling. Instead, she just shook her head.

"Take my money," he said to her.

Never in her life had her pride stung more than at that moment. She wanted her ranch, but taking money from Seth Connelly was something she simply couldn't do. "I can't."

Anger crossed Seth's face, but she sensed it wasn't directed at her. "I'm going to talk to this man. Give me your notes."

"I don't think it will help. He's a barracuda."

"I'm a lawyer, sweetheart. We're known for being sharks."

"I don't want to think of you swimming in the same water as that man."

"Wait in the car. I'll be right back."

"Seth—"

"Let me do this, Lynn. I owe your family a debt, and it's the only option you've left me."

"Okay." She handed over the folder that held all of the paperwork on the ranch's mortgage. She was careful not to let their fingers brush, remembering the sensation that had rocked her the last time. But more than anything, she wished she could lean against him. Rest against his tall, strong body and let her troubles recede if only for a few minutes. But Seth was a weakness she couldn't afford.

He opened the Jag's door for her and she watched him walk back into the bank. It was a cold, blustery day and the mountains in the distance seemed to look down on the little town of Sagebrush with wise eyes. She felt their stare and knew that the mountains weren't really censoring her for giving her trust blindly. But realizing that her friends and neighbors would know how foolish she'd been didn't make her feel confident that they wouldn't look on her the same way.

She tried to weigh her options objectively. If Matt were here, would he take Seth's money? She doubted it. Matt preferred relationships that were equal, and if he'd taken money from Seth, their friendship would be forever changed.

Should she call her brother? She knew he couldn't come home. He might offer to send some money, but she doubted he had the funds available to appease the bank and Mr. Cochran.

She couldn't sell the land in time to save the house, she knew. There simply wasn't enough time. She glanced down the town's main road. The diner she'd been working at seemed gloomy in the muted light of day. Her future didn't hold the shining promise it had during the summer when she'd been riding a mountain trail on the back of Thor, her gelded bay. Instead, she saw that choices—foolish choices—had led her to a point where she was going to have to give up all she owned.

His shoulders straight, his stride purposeful, Seth walked out of the bank like a man with too much confidence. A force unto himself, she thought. She watched him move and realized the feelings she'd felt for him at sixteen still throbbed within her. There was something about the aloof aura he projected that made her want to open her arms and pull him into her embrace. To show him in a very physical way—just a hug—that he wasn't alone in the world.

He opened the door and slid behind the wheel. Silently he passed her folder back to her, and Lynn set it in her lap and stared at him. He quirked one eyebrow at her.

"What happened?" she asked.

"You were right about Cochran."

Damn. She'd felt a twinge of hope when she'd seen Seth returning, but now she knew it had been irrational. Cochran wanted the McCoy land, and he wasn't going to be easily swayed from taking it.

"Thanks for trying, Seth."

"Hey, don't give up yet, sad eyes. I didn't say that I wasn't successful."

Her heart pounded so loudly that she couldn't hear for a minute. "Did you get him to agree to take payments from me?"

"Not exactly."

"What exactly is the deal you made?"

"It's kind of complex. I'm not sure the front seat of the car is the right place to talk about it."

"I can't wait. I need to know if my ranch is going to be mine next week or if I'm going to have to start living over the diner."

"Whatever happens with the ranch, I promise you, you will never live over the diner."

His words touched her as little else had in the last eighteen months she'd been totally on her own with the huge debt hanging over her head. "Thank you."

"Don't thank me yet. You might not like the solution."

"I'm not letting you pay it off."

"Cochran won't accept the money from me. Or let me buy the loan from him."

"I told you he was a barracuda."

"He made a tasty meal," Seth said.

"How did you get around him?"

"I presented the one solution even he couldn't refute."

Lynn waited for him to continue. Seth was one of the smartest and most successful men she knew. His solution was probably something she'd never considered because she'd never dealt in finance.

"I told him that we were getting married and that I'd be back in three days' time as your husband to pay off the loan."

Lynn blinked at him. "What did you say?"

"Marry me, Lynn?"

Four

The words had come out of nowhere. Marriage wasn't something he'd been looking for. He preferred the quiet solitude of his empty condo to large family gatherings. But the more he thought about marriage, the more strongly he was compelled to convince her to agree.

Besides, Cochran was being stubborn about the money. He wanted the McCoy land for his own and would stop at nothing to get it. But then he'd never tangled with Seth Connelly before.

"You can't be serious," she said. For the first time since he'd exited the bank, she didn't look as if she was going to cry.

"Why not?" He was a little offended that she

thought he was joking. He'd never proposed marriage to a woman before and frankly, he'd expected a different reaction.

Conversely, he was also relieved. She was his best friend's little sister. Which for some reason had never made her seem off limits even though it should have.

"We've never been friends," she said. They'd had what could only be called an adversarial relationship.

"We did just fine on that one summer night." He still remembered the setting sun and warm breeze. The feel of her slender, budding body in his arms and the taste of her strawberry-pink lips under his. The irrational urge to swear he'd protect her for the rest of his life.

"We were teenagers then, and even that didn't really work out. Marriage is a big step. I don't see us together for the rest of our lives. Besides I've heard tales about you from Matt."

He doubted she'd heard anything too strong. Matt was very protective of Lynn, which made Seth's position all the more precarious. He honestly believed the only solution was marriage, but he also knew he lusted after her and wanted to claim her for his own. Something that Matt wouldn't approve of.

"The front seat of my car isn't the place for this kind of conversation. Let's go back to the ranch and sort out the details."

"Sounds good to me."

Seth put the car in gear and backed out onto Main Street. He drove carefully down the thoroughfare, watching for pedestrians and being mindful of the speed limit. On the interstate he rode with the wind, but in the city he'd learned caution. You only had to see a victim of a hit-and-run at the hospital once to take your foot off the gas.

"It seems strange for you to be driving the speed limit down this road. You always flew like a bat out of hell."

"I've learned that speed isn't everything."

"I haven't," she said quietly.

"You've never been on the run. Only impulsive," he said, driving out of town toward the McCoy spread.

"I've let life direct me instead of directing my life."

"That sounds deep. Obviously you've been thinking about that for a long time."

"There's not been much to do lately except think."

"Well, don't dwell too much on your troubles. I'll help you sort them out."

"Seth, I'm not Cinderella waiting for her prince to come and rescue her from a life of manual labor."

"I know." Life would be so much easier if she were. But he knew that he wouldn't want her to pretend to be something she wasn't. Hadn't he been living an illusion for most of his adult life? The price was too steep to be paid by Lynn.

"I want to rescue myself."

"Even heroes sometimes need a hand."

"A hand—not a shove out of the way so that someone else can shoulder the burden."

"I've said it before, but damn you're stubborn." He turned into the McCoy driveway and pulled to a stop next to Lynn's truck. He made a mental note to call the town mechanic and have her truck tuned up after he convinced her to go to Vegas and marry him.

"Let's get inside and warm up. It's chilly today." Seth opened his door and went around to open Lynn's, but she was already getting out of the car.

"I'm not going to be impulsive about this," she warned.

"I've got all the time in the world. You're the one with the minutes ticking by."

She hurried away without saying anything, leaving him to regret his truthful words. But Seth had never been able to stomach even a polite lie. He'd spent too long being surrounded by the details of his birth.

He followed her into the kitchen. "I didn't intend for my words to hurt you."

"They didn't." She paused. "Look, I know you're right but the last time I trusted a man I ended up in this situation."

"I'm not any man."

"No, you're Matt's best friend."

"I'd like to think I'm your friend too, Lynn."

"Friendship is all we have?"

"Friendship and mutual love of this land."

"Why are you doing this?"

"Because you belong riding your horse not slinging hash in a diner."

"That's not much of a reason."

"Maybe I've always wanted to be a part of your family."

She sank into a kitchen chair and rested her head on her hands. She shouldn't look like this. He knew that God would never forgive him if he walked away from her and her troubles. To say nothing of how his best friend would react.

"Trust me on this, Lynn."

"I'm trying."

"What would reassure you?"

"I don't know. Would it be a real marriage?"

Yes, his libido screamed. But he knew that this was one time when he had to be ruled by his head and not his penis. Though he hated deceit of any kind, he knew that he couldn't stay married to his best friend's little sister. He was only doing this to help her out. No matter how much his body might clamor for something more, he was only going to be her husband on paper.

"Is there any other kind?" he asked.

"Sure, there are those business-deal ones."

"We'll have to see how it works out."

She stared at him, her eyes wide, her lower lip trembling. Damn, he'd learn to love cold showers if she didn't want to sleep with him. Hell, he'd marry her, fix this place and go back to Chicago before he forced himself on her. If and when Lynn came to him, it would be because she wanted to be in his arms.

Her words shook him to the core. "Will you marry me?"

"Yes."

Lynn wasn't sure she'd made the right choice. Every time she'd followed her impulsive nature, she'd ended up in trouble. And Seth wasn't a man she was immune to.

She'd wanted him longer than she'd admit to anyone. There was a part of her that was still sixteen and kissing him for the first time. She wondered how much he'd changed. Life had made her a different woman and Seth couldn't be the same man he'd been then.

Though he'd only been eighteen, there had always been a part of Seth that was mature. She wondered if maybe he didn't need her as much as she needed him. Perhaps, she thought, he needed someone to show him how to lighten up and enjoy life. That could be what she contributed to him.

Seth had promised her a real marriage, and though she wasn't ready for intimacy with him, they really had no choice. They had to marry—and quickly. But Seth had always struck her as a man who thought through every decision to the tiniest detail. Did he have another motive for marrying her?

"I'm not even sure what you have to do to get married," she said.

"Well, I don't know about other brides, but all you have to do is sit back and let me take care of the details."

"I'm not used to being passive, Seth."

"Try it this once."

"Okay."

Once he decided on a course of action, Seth moved at the speed of light. Lynn was still trying to come to grips with the fact that she didn't have to worry about losing the ranch.

"How does Vegas sound for a wedding?"

"Tacky."

He looked offended. "Hey, I'm a Connelly. We don't do anything less than classy."

"In Vegas?"

"Yes."

"Then I guess we'll get married in Nevada. When do we leave?"

"That depends on you. How long will it take you to pack?"

"Is this just an overnight trip?"

"The banks will be closed until Monday, so we'll stay through the weekend."

Though they'd decided to marry to save the ranch, they hadn't talked about emotions. Could she spend her life with a man who didn't love her? And why hadn't she thought about love earlier?

"Seth, I need to ask you something."

"Go ahead," he said.

Her heart was beating frantically. She looked at the

man who'd given her so much and knew no matter what happened, she'd do whatever she had to. Because she owed Seth.

"I don't know how to say this, so I'm just going to blurt it out. How do you feel about love?"

"I'm sorry?"

"I mean, we haven't talked about what our marriage will be like and I know we don't know each other well enough to be in love, but someday do you think I'm the kind of woman you could love?"

"I'm not going to delude you, Lynn. I think I could care deeply for you. As deeply as I do for my family in Chicago. But love? I've seen the dirtier side of that emotion and I'll never be that weak."

"Love's not a weakness."

"It is in Chicago, baby."

"But we're in Montana."

"For now."

She hadn't thought they'd live anyplace other than the ranch. "Does this mean we'd have to live in Chicago?"

"My job is there. We'll have to work out those details. Go get packed while I book a flight."

As she climbed up the stairs to her room, the house she'd lived in her entire life suddenly looked different. She knew it was because she was seeing it with new eyes. Before she got too hopeful, she reined herself in and tuned in to the part of her that worried that marrying Seth might be the biggest mistake she'd ever made.

"What are we going to do in Vegas for a few days?" she asked. "I'm not that big on gambling."

"I don't think we'll have a problem entertaining ourselves."

The warm look he gave her made her flush. She'd had a few torrid fantasies about Seth when they'd both been teens. Spending the day with him, seeing the man he'd matured into convinced her that Seth had grown into a man she could fall for easily. But her heart wasn't as trustworthy as she'd once believed, and life had a way of reminding you of those things.

It didn't stop the images of Seth making love to her in a showy Vegas hotel room. His muscled body moving over hers. She looked away, sure he could read the desire in her eyes.

She turned away before she did something she regretted. Something impulsive, like letting him see how easily she could fall in love with him. Something like smiling at him and dreaming of a lifetime of love when he had something else in mind.

She packed a duffel bag she used for overnight camping trips to the mountains. When she realized there was no suitable dress in her closet for a wedding, she suddenly worried that she wasn't good enough for Seth.

Not that he'd ever treated her as if she wasn't. But the women he knew no doubt had designer luggage and closets full of appropriate clothing for any occasion. She had jeans and a battered bag. She looked at herself in the mirror and almost changed her mind. She wasn't good at pretending to be something she wasn't.

She grabbed her bag and hurried back down the stairs. Seth was on the living-room couch, talking on his cellular phone and making notes on a legal pad. He looked up when she walked in and smiled at her. It was a reassuring expression that should have stilled the butterflies in her stomach but didn't.

"Can I get married in this suit?" she asked to change the subject.

He quietly ended his phone conversations. "No. We'll fly to Vegas tonight and get married there tomorrow. I'll arrange for a couple of wedding dresses to be sent to our suite for you to try on."

"Thank you. I've never been married before and I would like to wear a white dress."

"No problem, this is my first wedding too. But I think we should plan on it being our last."

"Yeah?"

"Yeah, I know we haven't had a chance to hammer out the details, but we can make this work. I'm not a quitter and neither are you."

"You're right."

"Are you sure about this, Lynn? I don't mind making a gift of the money."

She'd given her word and she wouldn't change her mind now. "Marriage is fine with me."

"I don't want to pressure you."

For the first time since Ronnie had left with her money, she found something funny. ‘‘You’re not.’’

‘‘This is your last chance to back out.’’

Maybe he’d changed his mind. ‘‘If you don’t want to marry me, Seth, just say so.’’

‘‘I want you more than any woman I’ve ever met.’’

His words brought sunshine to a soul that was weary and battered from its encounters with the opposite sex. She felt like a flower that had lain dormant for too long, and knew she owed Seth more than she could ever repay. They’d make a good marriage, she promised herself. She would do whatever necessary to ensure it.

The first flight to Vegas wasn’t until eight that night. By the time they’d finished packing, arranged for a neighbor to watch the animals and driven to the airport, they barely had thirty minutes to spare.

Lynn shared her concerns as they took their seats in the plane. ‘‘I’ve never flown before.’’

‘‘Are you scared?’’

‘‘A little. I mean I’m one of the people who stays behind and guards the homestead.’’

‘‘Not this time,’’ he said.

‘‘I’m not sure I’m ready to leave.’’

It struck him that Lynn wasn’t the type of woman he was used to. She hated change. She liked to stay in her safe routine, found something reassuring about it.

"I saw this special on *48 Hours* about engine failure in airplanes."

"What did it say?"

"That there was a defect the airlines didn't want you to know about."

"Lynn, relax. I fly all the time and haven't been in a single crash."

"There's always a first time."

"Okay, Ms. Sunshine, enough of those thoughts." He hailed a passing flight attendant and asked for two glasses of champagne.

She returned quickly with them and he handed one to Lynn. As she watched him warily, he had the strangest urge to tease her, to find a way to put her at ease—even though laughter created the strongest bonds he'd ever experienced. The last thing he needed was a stronger bond with her.

He raised his glass. "To the future of the McCoy Ranch."

Lynn tipped her glass to his and took a sip of her drink.

"Your turn."

"To arriving alive."

He narrowed his eyes at her and she gave him a mock kiss. Damn, he wanted it to be real. Needed it to be real. How was he going to keep this platonic, when he'd all but promised her that they'd have a real relationship? An adult relationship—one that would start before they returned to Montana.

Don't be sweet, he told Lynn in his thoughts. Keep

on being Matt's little sister and not the funny, attractive woman whom I want more than my next breath.

She broke into his thoughts. "Okay, a real toast. Ready?"

He nodded, not trusting his voice.

"To our life together."

She clinked her glass to his once again, but he couldn't drink. Her sincerity burned straight to the heart of the lie he'd given her for reassurance and now he had to live with the consequences. Had to find a way to make her see that the hurt he knew he'd have to deliver down the road would be for the best in the end.

Ah, hell. Just once couldn't life deal him a hand that was fairly easy to play? He knew that their life together would be relatively short. It affected him more than she'd ever know to realize that for once he wanted to hold on to someone, even though he'd learned it was better to let go.

They finished their champagne. Seth knew if he didn't put some barriers in place and fast, he was a goner. He'd lose Lynn, the McCoy Ranch and his best friend in one fell swoop. Because there was no way Lynn McCoy would ever be happy being a Connelly.

The only plan that had even a slight chance of working was an annulment. And it required only one thing—celibacy. He reminded himself as Lynn reached across his lap to retrieve her magazine and her breast brushed against his leg. Damn, he wanted to feel more of her. The cabin was dark and no one would have to know, he thought. But he'd know. And he was being noble.

Once the plane took off, Seth pulled out his laptop to work. He needed to focus on something other than the woman beside him. Even though he was on a leave of absence from his job, weird things had been happening in his family. His oldest brother was going to be King, his mom was connected to the mob and he'd left Chi-town to keep the Connellys safe. And he couldn't stay completely out of touch. Lynn read a magazine and then curled up in her seat. Seth powered down his computer, got a blanket from the flight attendant and draped it over her.

That small action should have been brotherly. And it was, he reassured himself. He'd preserved the wall around him by working and showing her that he couldn't—wouldn't—be able to be on for her 24/7.

She stirred in her sleep and shifted toward him, ending up with her head on his shoulder and her arm around his waist. In that instant, he'd gone from being an island to being a peninsula. In the scheme of things it wasn't a big change, but simply being connected to something shook Seth to the core.

Five

Vegas always felt like a second home to Seth. He'd always been fascinated by the world of bookies, con men and showgirls. His childhood had been kind of surreal—only son of a poor, single mom, then the son of a wealthy family. On his mom's side of the family he had a few cousins who worked here.

They were simple men who'd accepted the fact that they existed in the gray area of life. Something that Seth had always thought he'd be able to do if his father hadn't taken him in. The gray area wasn't bad. It was almost legal and didn't involve the innocent.

Unlike his current predicament. Lynn didn't look as if she'd come home. In her faded jeans and boots she looked fresh and…ah, hell, innocent. Dammit. He wasn't sure marrying her was the right thing to do. But once he'd settled on a course of action he didn't turn back.

His plan that had secmed so simple and easy in Montana was now more complex. The more time he spent in Lynn's company, the more he realized that keeping his hands off her was going to be nearly impossible. She drew him with her sharp wit and soft smiles. By turns she was a prickly, stubborn woman and then a sweet lady.

The cab pulled to a stop in front of one of the Merv Griffin hotel/casinos. Night had fallen and the Strip was resplendent with lights and tourists. Lynn stood on the sidewalk as he tipped the cabdriver.

"Wow! I've never seen so much..."

Sin? he thought, but didn't say it. He didn't want to point out the differences between them if she didn't see them. He knew Vegas suited him like a one-of-a-kind leather jacket, and the feel of it was soft and smooth.

"What?" he asked, taking her by the elbow to lead her into the hotel. She could easily have walked inside without him guiding her but he wanted to touch her, even if it was through layers of clothing. In fact, he wanted nothing so much as to strip away the layers of cloth and caress the woman underneath.

"I'm trying to find the right word."

She was smart. She'd figure it out sooner or later and he didn't believe in lying.

"Sin, lights, tourists."

She laughed. It was a sweet sound and he stopped to smile down at her. "You sound so cynical."

"Maybe I am."

"No, you're not." She touched his cheek, and met his gaze full on. In her eyes was the promise of something he'd never experienced before. Something he'd never seen in anyone's eyes as they looked at him.

He was struck by the twin urges to protect and ravage this woman. This petite blonde who was his opposite in every way. He took her hand and held it firmly in his own, leading her into the hotel. The sensual scent of flowers and an essence that was only Lynn surrounded him. His groin hardened as they approached the concierge desk.

The better part of him—his rational mind—told him he should contact Matt and get as far away from Lynn as possible. He should take the first flight back to Chicago.

But his body was making a stronger argument than his mind, and for the first time in his life Seth was taking what he wanted. He wasn't being shaped at military school into someone worthy of the Connelly name. He was just Seth. And Lynn accepted him as such, which was as much a turn-on as her sexy body and long blond hair.

"I was going to say opulent."

"Merv does know how to do a hotel the right way."

"I feel so out of place."

"You're not," he said.

"It's just that I know I come from a run-down ranch in Montana and these people look like they were born here."

"Vegas is all illusion, Lynn. Don't forget that."

"What do you mean?"

"What you see isn't what you really get. What you see is a mirage."

"I see you," she said softly.

Her words cut to his soul, and for a minute the reality of what he was doing struck him. He was marrying her to repay a debt and he knew she wouldn't want that. But he wasn't turning back. Couldn't let her go at this late time.

"And I see you. Just remember that what we are here is an illusion."

"You look like you belong here," she said.

He nodded. "I know."

As they moved forward in the line, Seth wanted to put his arm around her to keep her close by his side but didn't. He wasn't a needy man. He was solitary by nature and experience and he was savvy enough to know trouble when it looked at him. Even if it was only through Lynn's violet eyes.

Those eyes took in everything around them, assessing, deciding. "It's different but I think I like it."

"What do you like the most?"

"I haven't experienced everything you promised yet."

Her words went through him like a gambler through his winnings. She wanted him. He wondered how quickly they could get married tonight, because he needed her in his bed. He needed to make her his in an elemental way.

"Want to get married now?" he asked, his voice guttural.

Her eyes widened. He thought he saw maybe a hint of fear in them but she smiled slowly. "You promised me a white dress."

There was hope in her voice and he knew that she had to feel a little vulnerable without her family. It struck him that Lynn and he weren't all that different. They were both essentially alone in this world. "I always keep my promises."

"I know you do, Seth."

"Not everyone does," he said without thinking. His father hadn't said a word when it was revealed that his mother had once again tried to betray the Connellys; but Seth had seen the coldness in Grant's eyes and knew once again he'd let them down.

"Then they don't know the real Seth Connelly."

"Sometimes I don't think that I do."

She leaned up and kissed him on the cheek. "He's an honorable man who lives by his own code."

"Next, please," called the concierge.

Seth walked over to check in, aware of Lynn's gaze on him the entire time. Her words echoed in his mind and he felt a twinge of doubt at their union. There was no way he could live up to her expectations of him. But a part of him wanted to.

The next afternoon Lynn knew she'd made a big mistake as soon as she held the first wedding dress. Seth had gone to the other room to make some business phone calls, so she was alone in the luxurious bedroom. The carpet was plush under her feet, the champagne was expensive to the taste and the music was refined and elegant in the background.

She knew then that she was in real danger of buying into the whole reality. How could she remember that Seth thought this was all an illusion, while she held a dress that dreams were made of? She couldn't pretend he was nothing more to her than a business partner in the ranch when he looked at her as he had in the lobby.

Or when he showed her his vulnerability. Seth had never been an easy boy to know. When the rest of her brother's friends were open and obvious, Seth was guarded. He'd always enthralled her.

Her heart beat a little faster when he knocked on the door.

"How's it coming? Have you picked a dress yet?"

Tears burned the back of her eyes. As a little girl she'd dreamed of doing this with her mother. The pain still felt sharp. Her mother was gone, her brother was deep undercover and she was with a man who warned her that he didn't believe in love.

She knew without a doubt that she did. And she knew, as she stared at herself in the mirror, that she could fall in love with Seth Connelly with very little trouble.

The world tipped on its axis.

"Lynn, are you okay?"

There was a caring in his words. She didn't know if it was concern for his best friend's sister or for the woman he'd asked to marry him. And were those two people different for him?

Though he'd been subtle, she knew he desired her. But did he want the woman as well as the body? That question mocked her as she let the dress fall to the padded chaise. She couldn't marry him unless he wanted to marry her for herself.

Not because Matt wasn't here to rescue her. Not because Seth needed something to take his mind off whatever had sent him from Chicago. Not because lust ran rampant through their bodies.

"No, I'm not," she said, opening the door.

Seth had shed his jacket and tie while he'd been on the phone. His dark hair was ruffled as if he'd speared his fingers through it, and his collar was open, revealing his dark skin. He looked tired and weary and she wanted to open her arms to him. To offer him a place to rest from the crazy world.

"How'd your phone call go?"

"As well as expected," he said.

"Can I help?"

"You are."

"I don't see how."

"You're giving me a chance to prove I'm more than what my parents made me."

"Seth, what demons are you running from?"

"Not the kind you'd ever want to know."

She wanted to touch him but sensed his control hung by a thin thread. Insight was late coming but she realized that Seth needed her as much as she'd needed his rescue and his money. He needed her to help him through whatever family problems had once again sent him to Montana.

"What's wrong with the dresses?" he asked.

"Nothing. They're beautiful."

He nodded and waited for her to continue. But somehow she couldn't bring herself to say out loud that she wasn't right for the dresses. Or that she wasn't right for this suite. Because then he'd know what she really meant—she wasn't right for him.

"Those dresses are too much."

"I asked my sister Tara to pick them out. She made a few calls from Chicago. So I'm sure they're just right."

"Maybe for a Connelly."

"Which you will soon be."

"I'm trying not to buy into the illusion."

"What illusion? We really are getting married."

"I don't want to become your wife because you need a distraction."

"Hell, that's not why I'm marrying you."

"Then why are you?"

Silence. The dead quiet in the room seeped through her layers of clothing, chilling her to her soul. There was no reason why he was marrying her. No reason at all except that he knew Matt would want the ranch when he got out of the service.

"Because I needed rescuing," she said.

"Partly. There's something about you, Lynn. There has always has been something that entrances me."

"In your youth it made you want to play pranks on me."

"Only to keep alive the premise that you were still a kid and I was a man."

"I'm not sure you were a man at eighteen."

"Funny, I've felt like one since I was eight."

His words struck a chord and she realized that he did want from her something other than a bedmate. Trying to put it into words wasn't working for him, but his gray eyes were sincere.

She closed the distance between them. Wrapping her arms around his waist, she rested her head against his chest. His arms stayed by his sides and she wondered if she'd misread him.

She felt him sigh, and then tentatively his arms enclosed her. She never wanted to leave this spot, she realized. His heart beat steadily under her ear, his warmth surrounded her, and for this one moment she felt as if he cared.

The cool sophistication Seth had learned to imitate from his brothers and stepmom disappeared. He finally had Lynn where he'd fantasized about having her. Though he knew he shouldn't let this embrace go beyond a brief hug, instinct took over.

He lifted her face toward his. Those luscious lips of hers, free of makeup, tempted him more than any of the glamorous women he knew in Chicago. Her skin felt likc silk tu his fingers, softer than anyone he'd ever touched.

He wanted to linger but was afraid she'd bolt. And he needed to know how she tasted more than he needed his next breath.

The iron control he'd exerted since he'd first entered military school was the only thing that allowed him to slowly lower his head. His gut urged him to crush his mouth to hers. To plunder it for the sweetness that only she could provide, and drink until his thirst was quenched. Suddenly it felt like years since he'd had a woman in his arms.

Lynn's violet eyes were wide open, watching every move he made. Her gaze was welcoming but distant. As if she feared this embrace as much as she wanted it.

Later he knew he'd regret this, but he closed the small gap between them. Her lips were full and warm, pliant under his own, and there was no awkwardness to the embrace. He slid his tongue across the seam of her mouth and she sighed.

Her mouth opened and he felt her invitation to come deeper. She tasted of something elemental. Something he'd never tasted in an embrace before. Something that was Lynn.

Her tongue reciprocated, tasting his mouth and setting his hormones ablaze. In a rush he hardened uncomfortably against the inseam of his trousers.

He slid his hands down her back, settling them on her backside. She adjusted her body to cradle his erection. Ah, yes, he thought, here was what he needed. What they both needed to distract them from the vulnerability that they both felt.

Though Seth wouldn't admit it to a living soul, he needed comfort from Lynn now. He needed her to marry him because for the first time he looked at the future and it was cold and empty.

He groaned at the rightness of it. He tore his mouth from hers. Her eyes were wide and questioning. Lynn had never felt more fragile to him. Her slender shoulders under his hands made him feel big and manly, a stark contrast to the ethereal woman in his arms.

Her lips were full and welcoming, her tongue shy but knowing. Almost like Lynn herself. Tentative were her touches and he wondered if she was afraid of him or herself.

Leaning back against the wall, he pulled her even closer. He lifted her thigh so that he could press his arousal more fully against the center of her body. She moaned a deep throaty sound that almost made him lose control.

Her fingers tunneled through his hair and she pulled his mouth to hers. She kissed like someone who was on the verge of orgasm, and he didn't want her to ever stop. With his hands on her hips, he urged her to move against him. Quicker until her breath caught.

Her nails dug into his biceps and he knew she hung on the precipice. He moved his hips, rubbing against her with more strength than before, and she opened her mouth on a gasp.

The sound was fire to his body that was already hotter than the sun. "Like that?"

"Oh, Seth, why does this feel so good?" she asked.

She slid her hands under his clothing. Her fingers were long and cool against his back and he wanted her touch somewhere else. Her words barely registered. He could think only of her touching him where he needed her most.

"More, baby?"

"Yes..."

He did it again and she arched against him at the end of his thrust. Damn, the clothing was in the way. He reached between them to free himself, and as his hand rubbed across the center of her desire, she shuddered in his arms. He held her trembling body.

Her face was flushed, her eyes tightly closed and Seth had never seen anyone look lovelier. Her climax had brought him to the edge, but he was still hungry for Lynn. Hungry for her body clenching around his. The next time orgasm put that look on her face, he vowed to be hilt deep inside her.

Hopefully the next time wouldn't be that long from now. He lifted her in his arms and carried her to the king-size bed that dominated the room. Other than a small wedge of sunlight that peeked out from between the black-out drapes, the rest of the room was in shadows.

Seth felt the comfort of that dim room in the same way that Vegas had welcomed him. He was at home in the shadows. Always had been. Even in the big Connelly house, he spent a majority of the time hiding.

He wondered if he was hiding from more than Lynn in this darkened room. He settled her in the center of the bed and reached for her shirt. A knock on the door of the suite stopped him. That was probably the lady Tara had arranged to show Lynn veils.

Lynn sat up on the bed. Even in the shadows he knew she'd changed her mind. She was saved by the bell and he was damned by it.

"Second thoughts?" he asked. His body throbbed in time to his racing pulse. She was so close he could smell her sweetness, and he didn't know if the veil lady would be enough to keep him from having her.

He should have taken her where they'd been standing. But Lynn deserved a bed when they made love, not a hurried coupling against the wall.

"And third and fourths," she said.

"Not tonight, eh?"

"I know it sounds silly. But we're getting married tonight and I want our wedding night to be special."

"What if we're not compatible?" he asked.

"Please, if we were any more compatible, this room would have gone up in flames."

"I almost did," he said.

"I did. Thank you."

He knew that she probably wanted to escape. She'd been so vulnerable a few minutes ago, and the fact that she wanted to wait made him realize she probably still didn't trust him. He didn't blame her.

But he wanted to hold her for a few minutes. Hold her for just a short while here in the shadows where no one could see him. Hold her now while it was safe to do so, because he'd only just realized that she had the power to burst through his outer walls and see straight to his heart. In the shadows maybe she wouldn't realize the control he'd been powerless to stop from giving her.

Six

Seth left the suite once the lady from the bridal shop arrived. Lynn didn't know where he was going but she didn't try to stop him. They both needed some fresh air. Especially Seth.

If that knock hadn't sounded on the door when it had, she would have made love with him. She still wished she had, but she knew that what she would have seen as a meeting of the souls, Seth would have viewed as physical gratification. After her last adult relationship, she needed it to mean more to him.

She didn't think that mere hours would make that big a difference, but she was determined to make the most of that time to show him they had more than a past filled with mischief and a present filled with hot sex.

All of the dresses were lovely and showy. The kind of gowns that only a woman who was confident of herself and her femininity could wear. Lynn freely acknowledged that Ronnie had wounded something very feminine in her when he left, but she didn't think she could have worn those dresses in any circumstances. They weren't her.

She'd pretended to be someone she wasn't with Ronnie and that had backfired. The only way she'd survive a lifetime with Seth was to be honest about who she was.

"Do you have anything a little...plainer?"

The saleswoman looked her over with a practiced eye. "I have a new Vera Wang that might work. I'll have it sent right up."

"Thanks. These are all so pretty but they're not me."

"I think you're right."

The saleswoman left, and while she was gone, Lynn tried on veils, choosing a simple one that flattered her slim features and long hair.

After the assistant returned with two dresses, Lynn tried the first one on and fell in love. Even the ladies from the boutique smiled knowingly when she fastened the back of the dress. It was simple yet feminine and made Lynn feel as if she was a fairy-tale princess for the first time in her life.

The ladies left, taking the extra dresses with them, and Lynn knew she should change out of her wedding gown but couldn't. Though night was falling on Vegas, only a small lamp illuminated the suite's main room. Lights spread out under the window for as far as she could see. And she saw something else—her reflection in the floor-to-ceiling glass.

She spun around and then moved closer to study that woman. Was that really Lynn McCoy?

Seth entered the suite without knocking. She pivoted to face him, not wanting him to see her gawking at herself. His shirt was open at the collar and his suit jacket flung over his shoulder. Though he looked at ease, there was nothing casual about him. An intensity burned in his eyes that made her tingle in the most delicious way.

He paused just inside the doorway. The look on his face was unreadable. She hoped it was okay that she'd picked out a dress on her own and not one that his sister had selected.

Silence grew and she started to forget that in this dress she looked like a fairy princess. She started to feel like the dusty cowgirl who'd come in from the range. She started to remember that Seth wasn't her Prince Charming though he'd saved her ranch. He didn't want her.

"It's bad luck for you to see my dress. You should have knocked."

He closed the door and crossed the suite. "Honey, I've had Lady Luck on my side most of my life and have yet to feel lucky."

"I never have."

He moved closer to her and she could see that he

wasn't unaffected by her dress. His erection strained against his zipper. His reaction to her caused a definitely equal reaction in her body. Heat pooled in her center, and her nipples beaded up against the satin of her dress. The design made it impossible for her to wear a bra and right now she was glad of it.

"Maybe it's time things changed for both of us," he said, brushing his finger along her cheek.

Though he was not a soft man, there was a gentle side to Seth that she doubted he even realized he had. But he touched her so carefully sometimes that he made her feel as though she was the most important thing in his world.

"I hope they can." In fact, she'd placed her future on that sentiment.

"Turn around so I can get the full effect of the dress."

"Don't you want to wait and be surprised at the wedding?"

"Turn," he ordered.

She pivoted and knew he saw her bare back. In the reflection of the window she watched him reach out as if to touch her and then pull back. He didn't trust something. Her?

"Seth?"

"Yes," he said, his voice husky. She finished turning and saw that his eyes were shuttered and his hands jammed deep in his pockets.

"I let you dodge the subject in the car but I think we need to hammer out those details now."

"It's late, Lynn. I just spent the last two hours in the bar, reminding myself that you're Matt's sister. But I have to tell you all I can see when I close my eyes is the way you looked when you came in my arms earlier."

She flushed. "I…"

"Honey, I know this situation isn't one you can control and you don't like that. Hell, I don't like it. But I can't talk to you right now when all I can think about is that bed in the other room and how lovely you'd look lying on it."

In her heart she'd believed he cared for her, even if it was only the warmth of his friendship with her brother spilling over. But she realized as he stood next to her radiating sexual energy that it was only lust.

"If we have sex, can we talk after?" she asked.

Taking a step back, she was ready to bolt, but he caught her hand, stopping her escape. She needed to get out of this dress, because she'd bought into the illusion even though he'd warned her not to. Her eyes burned. She had to escape and quick.

"Dammit, Lynn. When you and I do go to bed together, it's going to be more than sex."

Carefully she slid her hand out of his grasp. "I wish I could believe that."

Let her go, he told himself.

Women were more trouble than they were worth. He'd learned that lesson more than once since he'd been born. He was the cynic here, he thought.

Lynn was the one with the faith in love and happy-ever-after. If she was running away, then they were in more trouble than he'd thought. Maybe he should end this now. The money was being wired to him and he'd be able to pick up the cashier's check when they checked out. The McCoy ranch would soon be safely in the hands of the McCoys again. A few calls to some colleagues of his had netted an expert in ranch management who was on his way to Montana to take over the day-to-day tasks so that Lynn could enjoy the ranch.

Yet he couldn't let her go. Or was it *wouldn't?* He admitted to himself that he liked the way she made him feel. As if he was her hero instead of the mischief-maker who'd brought disgrace to his family. The sensation was heady and he never wanted it to end.

But he knew that Lynn needed more. And he wasn't certain he had that much left to give. He needed to remember that or else he'd find himself alone again. And without a refuge to run to.

He needed the McCoys—not just his friendship with Matt but this new thing he had with Lynn. He knew it was more than the hard-on in his pants.

His hormones urged him to go after her, but his heart that had learned to be wary told him to stay where he was. Lynn McCoy had way too much stubbornness and pride but not enough ego. No man would want only sex from her.

She represented the girl next door to him. She was his secret fantasy because he'd always been surrounded by showgirls and sophisticated women. He actually craved someone all-American. Even if he'd never met her brother, he'd still treat Lynn with respect. She normally exuded a kind of self-assurance that demanded it.

"Honey, stop."

She paused on the edge of the shadows in the bedroom. Her white dress glowed in the soft lamplight and her back was so stiff and straight she'd have passed inspection at the military school he'd attended as an adolescent.

"Don't call me honey in that soft voice, Seth. I know you don't mean it but it sounds like you care, and I'm trying real hard right now not to buy into the illusion."

Damn. He'd hurt her. He could tell that from her voice and the way she wouldn't look at him. Lynn always faced her opponent in battle yet now she was retreating.

"I do care." She'd be surprised to know how much.

"Only until I try to get to know the real you. Then you push me away."

"The real me. I'm not even sure who that man is anymore."

"Give me a break. He's a successful lawyer from a wealthy family. What's not to know?"

If only that were the whole story. He didn't want to sound like a sad sack whining because his mother didn't love him. But Angie's betrayal had left a gap deep inside him that made him question certain cornerstones he'd always taken for granted. "Something like being betrayed by your biological mother might make a man question who he believes he is.''

She turned to face him. Moisture made her eyes glassy but she was concerned now. Concerned about him. Part of him realized he'd known she would be; for all her toughness, there was something very soft about her. He realized that was part of her appeal. Once he'd set on the course of saving the ranch, it was safe for him to acknowledge the attraction he'd felt for her for a long time. And unless he'd lost all of his perception where women were concerned, she felt the same.

''Want to talk about it?'' she asked.

The compassion almost undid him. Survival depended on one thing, he reminded himself. Being able to stand alone. And confiding in Lynn wouldn't enable him to do that.

''Not really,'' he said, coming closer to her. He could smell her floral perfume. It swept over him in a wave, reminding him of how long ago spring was and leaving him feeling alone and cold in its wake.

She held her hand up to stop him. ''I can't deal with this right now. Getting married without any family around me is taking all the control I have.''

''What do you want from me?'' he demanded. He was rock hard with an erection that showed no signs of waning. Emotionally he'd had more than he could take for one day. And she wasn't through with him yet.

''Understanding.''

''You've got it.''

''Compassion?''

He nodded.

"Affection?"

He understood where she was coming from. Marrying someone for reasons other than love went against the grain, against the fairy tale that all young girls grow up believing in. "You are the only woman I've asked to marry me. That should tell you something."

"It does but I need more. I'm looking to you to provide some reassurance."

He'd never shirked from the truth and didn't hedge now. "I care for you. I always have."

"It's more than affcction for my family because we took you in when you needed a safe harbor?"

"Yes. I wouldn't marry you if I didn't want you. My desire for you has nothing to do with that."

"What does it involve?"

"Raging lust and very little thought."

She gave him a half smile that said she understood. He closed the gap between them, held her in his arms. Though he wanted to ravage her body, to pull that fantasy bridal gown from her body, more than that he needed to comfort her. To give her some reassurance with his body that he could never offer in words.

But there was no time. "We're getting married in two hours, then having dinner with some cousins of mine."

"I don't think I'm up to a meeting with your family."

"You'll like these guys, I promise."

"And you always keep your promises, right?"

He nodded.

"Then promise me this marriage isn't a mistake."

He brushed his lips against her cheek and stepped back because he couldn't keep holding her and still get them downstairs in time to be married.

"I promise this marriage won't be a mistake."

"I'm going to hold you to it," she said and walked into the other room to finish getting ready.

Seth took the tuxedo bag from the hall closet where he'd asked the bellman to deliver it earlier and went to the shower. He tried not to admit the importance of what he'd just promised, because he knew he had no way to make that promise real unless he let Lynn inside his soul—and there was no way he'd ever be that vulnerable.

They were married in a small wedding chapel on the sixth floor of the hotel. The ceremony was discreet and subtly sophisticated with none of the garishness one would expect of a Vegas wedding. It still didn't feel right to Lynn. Her only family in the world was far away, unreachable, and she sensed he wouldn't approve of her marrying Seth.

Matt was the only one who knew that they'd kissed that long-ago night. In those days he would've been thrilled to have Seth as a brother-in-law, but Seth's rogue ways were too much for Lynn, and Matt had warned her to stay away from the Chicago bad boy.

If only Matt could see Seth now. Seth had done his best to make the ceremony as low-key and comfortable for her as he could. He wasn't the young hood he'd been in the past; he wasn't even the calmly confident lawyer she'd glimpsed at the bank yesterday.

He was a mature man taking care of his own. Lynn was touched beyond words.

When the photographer posed them for pictures, she broke down. Her parents were long gone, her brother's life was separate from hers and her future was tied to a man who'd warned her not to buy into the illusion.

The only illusion that she was even close to falling for was Seth. Since the officiant had pronounced them man and wife, her heart beat quicker. She knew she was dangerously close to believing that Seth was her forever man.

He never had been. Since the first time they'd met, he'd been on the run. Why would he change now? Why would he stay in Montana when she was the only thing holding him there?

Seth dismissed the photographer and witnesses from the room. Pulling a snowy-white handkerchief from his pocket, he dried her eyes. "What's wrong?"

She took a deep breath and tried to find the words to tell him what she was feeling. But they wouldn't come. There were some things she couldn't say to Seth—actually quite a few—and telling him that she was falling in love with him was one of them.

"I don't know," she said, hedging.

"Changed your mind already?" His demeanor was stiff and unsure, almost as if he'd expected her to back out of their agreement. Thinking about his mother and what she knew of his past, she didn't blame him for thinking the worst of her.

She wouldn't do that to him. Seth was important

to her. More important than he'd ever know and not just because he'd saved her ranch from the bank.

"No," she said. "It's just this isn't what I expected." Lynn knew her words misled him, because Seth had exceeded her expectations.

"I know."

If only he really did know. But her days of hitching her wagon to a distant star were over. She was standing on her own this time. But why did he have to look so appealing, so strong, and his shoulders so damn able to carry her burdens?

"Weddings have always kind of creeped me out," he said.

"Why?"

"I don't know. Maybe because my parents were never married."

She inhaled and closed her eyes. She didn't want him to think he'd made a mistake this soon. She had to stop reacting like an emotional invalid. Though in essence she knew she was.

"How did you feel about that?"

"When I was little and lived with my mom, it seemed as if no one had a normal family. We all ran together on the streets. The next generation of punks."

"No one would ever have called you a punk, Seth."

"You're wrong. My father did the first time he saw me."

"Mine didn't."

"Hey, I'd had a semester of military school. I'd lost some of my edge."

"I don't think you lost it. You may have smoothed it out a bit but it was still there when we met."

He nodded. "I know this isn't your dream wedding, but if you keep crying I'm going to have a hard time convincing everyone that you wanted to marry me."

"Oh, Seth," she said with a weak smile.

"Are you okay now?"

"Yes."

"Good. I'll call the photographer back in.... Are you sure it isn't the thought of meeting my cousins?"

"No."

"I know they can be a little intimidating. In fact, they've used it to their advantage over the years."

"Are you trying to tell me something about them?"

"I don't want to mislead you, Lynn. My father's side of the family is upstanding and well respected. My mom's family— Let's just say they aren't."

"That doesn't bother me."

"I'm glad because I'm more at home with these guys than with the Connellys in Chicago sometimes."

"Why is that?"

"I've never really thought about it."

"Maybe if you did, you'd stop running."

He cradled her close to his chest and she could hear his heart beat under her ear. It was reassuring.

"You okay now?" he asked.

She took a deep breath. "I will be."

He tilted her face up toward his. His eyes compelling her to meet his gaze. She wondered if he'd kiss her, because more than anything in the world she wanted his lips on hers.

"I promise you that fate wants us to be together."

His words rocked her, made her feel secure in a way she'd never felt before. He set her away from him and walked to let the photographer back in.

Seth had made her feel special in a way no man had before. He valued her opinion and listened to her when she talked. The only other man to ever do that had been her brother and that was solely because she was the only one on the ranch for him to talk to.

Seth returned and they were posed once again in front of the altar. The photographer had them smile at the camera and then asked them to face each other. Lynn looked up into Seth's eyes and knew she'd made the right decision. Despite the fact that Seth wasn't from her hometown, he was solid and dependable and she needed both.

Seven

Nearly an hour later, Lynn still hadn't recovered her equilibrium. Seth's cousins Paul and Michael were two brothers who seemed ill at ease in her presence. But were genuinely fond of Seth. The brothers were at least five years older than her new husband.

''Congratulations on your marriage,'' Paul said.

''You're getting a great guy,'' Michael said.

They embraced Seth in turn, and when they all were seated, Seth ordered a bottle of champagne. Paul and Michael treated her with respect and called her ma'am. And though Seth said they were related to him, she could see little resemblance. Aside from the fact that you had a feeling these two didn't lose many fights and neither did Seth.

Paul was the more outgoing of the two and kept her entertained with stories of the showgirls he knew. Lynn had a moment's realization that there was an entire world of which she knew nothing about.

It also made her realize that Seth's life in Chicago was probably as different from Montana and her daily routine as showgirls and slot machines. Doubt assailed her. Had she taken the easy way out of her problems instead of making a logical decision?

A waitress came and took their order and Lynn was surprised when Paul ordered in French. Ruefully she reminded herself not to make snap judgments. A quick glance at Seth showed he knew that Paul had surprised her.

After the waitress had left, conversation flowed around the table. Lynn tried to keep track of it but had a hard time focusing. So much had happened in the last thirty-six hours. This was the first time she'd sat down, and suddenly she was overwhelmed.

Michael got a page before they'd ordered dessert and made a quick call on his cell phone, after which both brothers soon excused themselves.

Lynn was disappointed to see them go for two reasons. Firstly because Seth seemed so relaxed around them, as if he forgot his troubles for just a little while—something he hadn't been able to do in her presence. And secondly, the brothers were a barrier between her and her new husband. The man who warned her not to buy into the illusion and then said things like "Fate wants us to be together."

"Paul and Michael are an interesting pair. Are you close to them?" she asked.

"I fly out here twice a year to see them. We roamed the streets together as youths."

"What does that mean?"

"Skipping school."

"What was that like?"

"It was incredibly scary when I was eight. But then by the time I turned nine it wasn't so bad."

She couldn't imagine any mother leaving her child alone for that amount of time, especially at so young an age. "Didn't your mother object?"

"No. She was busy."

"Working?"

"I guess you could call it that. She does whatever my uncle tells her to. They told her I'd be okay with Paul and Michael and she believed them."

"Were you?"

"Yes. The three of us always got along."

She sipped her cappuccino and tried not to let Seth seep past any further barriers. But it was hard. The more she learned about him the harder it was to resist him physically and emotionally. There was a maternal part of her that wanted to cradle him in her arms and comfort the small boy who'd been cast out alone. But then there was the elemental woman who wanted to cradle him in a totally different way. He confused her.

Closing her eyes, she tried to come up with something to say that wouldn't make him more appealing.

That wouldn't reveal more of the man who didn't seem to fit his world-weary image.

"I have a silly question," she said.

"Go ahead."

"Why are Paul's and Michael's shoulders so big? I'd think it was genetic but yours aren't that large. I've seen wrestlers who'd look puny next to them." Paul and Michael both had dark hair and a muscular build.

"Should I be offended?"

She blushed. "I didn't mean you looked small."

"Lynn, you're going to give me a complex."

"I doubt it."

"I don't," he said, meeting her gaze. His eyes promised darkly sensual things.

"Tell me about your cousins."

"Most of it is muscle and the rest is a shoulder holster."

"I can't believe your cousins are in law enforcement."

"More like enforcement."

"I don't understand."

"They work for a loan shark. And when people don't pay up, they track them down."

"Not exactly a tame line of work."

"No, it isn't."

He stared at the seats vacated by his cousins as if seeing someone who wasn't there. "Sometimes I wonder if I wouldn't have been happier leading that kind of life."

"I can't imagine you being satisfied working for someone else."

"I do every time I enter a courtroom."

"Yes, but you do it on your own terms."

"So do they."

"But your code of honor would be tarnished, Seth."

"Do you really think I have a code of honor?"

"I wouldn't be in Vegas with you if you didn't."

"Thank you."

Though she'd been warned she felt reality and illusion meld as the jazz trio played "Our Love Is Here To Stay" while Seth paid the bill. She looked at Seth, feeling the world tip on its axis, and saw not the boy she'd had a crush on, not the man who'd walked into her diner a couple of days earlier, but the man she'd married and who'd come to mean more to her than she'd ever imagined he would.

Lifting Lynn into his arms as the elevator doors closed softly behind them wasn't something his mind ordered but something his gut did. There was an emotion in her dark violet eyes that made him want to be the Prince Charming he saw mirrored there. Even if he knew it was only an illusion.

Seth knew he was going to pay for this night for a long time. He'd originally fooled himself into marrying Lynn by pretending he could make her his in name only. As he shifted her in his arms to carry her across the threshold of their suite, he knew he couldn't.

"Why are you carrying me?" she asked, her breath fanning his neck and starting a chain reaction that ended in his groin.

"For luck?" Maybe if he said it out loud his body would believe it. But he knew good fortune was the last reason why he was holding her in his arms. Raging lust beat it hands down.

He'd already crossed boundaries that he shouldn't have. He'd already taken steps that would drive Matt from his life. He'd already condemned himself, he thought. And the boy who'd been raised to believe that the law was something to be skated around asked himself, why not go all the way?

But for all her spunkiness, there was something innocent about Lynn McCoy, and he wasn't about to destroy it. He didn't want to do whatever that stockbroker on his way to Los Angeles had done to her. He somehow wanted to be better than he really was for her.

The fire that she'd lit in his body hadn't been extinguished by anything as mundane as dinner and conversation. Her insight and keen understanding had in fact fanned the flames. For the first time he felt like he knew who the real Seth Connelly was, and that scared him because it felt as though he'd only found the knowledge with Lynn.

She wouldn't stay.

Women never did.

Especially once he started needing them.

He knew then that he could never need Lynn. Already she affected him more strongly than anyone else he'd dated before. This insanity had to end, he thought, before it destroyed them both. But he was just a man. And temptation was stronger tonight.

"I've always dreamed of being carried by a strong, handsome man." She looked up at him with stars in her eyes. With her slender fingers she caressed his neck and jaw. Involuntarily he clenched it.

He'd never been touched by a woman except for sex. Lynn's touch now was a caress that was foreign to him and he resented that.

He didn't want to feel, but she made his emotions churn like never before. First he was her brother's best friend, then hers, then he was the man who could rescue the ranch. But the man he could never be was her husband.

There was nothing he wouldn't give to be just that man right now. He shifted her again, realizing how fragile she was in his arms. Realizing the precious gift she'd given him when she'd agreed to marry him. Realizing that despite his physical strength, at this moment the real power was in her hands.

Those strong, slender hands that touched him so softly. Like he was a man who'd never seen the seamier side of life. Like he was a man who'd fulfill her dreams. Like he was a man who could be a hero—her hero.

Damn. She tempted him. She lay so trustingly in

his arms, watching him with that intent gaze that reminded him that she'd been on an emotional roller coaster since the moment they'd met. Her breast was less than an inch from his fingers and though he knew he shouldn't, he caressed her on the sly, the way he would have palmed treasure from a store in his youthful shoplifting days.

She wrapped her arms around his neck. "If you say so. Are you sure this is all just for luck?"

He knew there was more than luck involved with him carrying her. But no one liked to look too closely at their own weaknesses. He was no different.

"What else could there be?" he asked carefully. He'd tried to bank his desire for her and stop touching the full globe of her breast. But knew that he'd done a poor job of it.

Probably because he wasn't paying as close attention to that detail as he should. But when he closed his eyes, all he saw was the way she'd shuddered with her climax in his arms.

"I don't know. But it might have something to do with the way you're touching me," she said.

He hesitated outside their suite door, feeling her nipple bead under his fingers that had wandered farther than they should have. He'd give up his fancy car, his career as a lawyer and the Connelly name to have her naked in his arms. He should be getting out the key card, carrying her over the threshold and taking a very cold shower. Instead he looked into her eyes and saw desire mirrored there. Saw need and hunger and couldn't quite stop so soon.

"How am I touching you?" he asked, brushing a butterfly kiss against her hairline.

"I'm not sure," she said, though her fingers in his hair belied her words, as did her lips against his neck and the teasing brush of her teeth against his skin.

He shuddered. They had to get out of the hallway. He had to get her out of his arms before he did something he'd regret even longer than he regretted the fact that he'd never really be a Connelly, even if his father had invited him into the fold.

"What does it feel like?" he asked against her ear. She shivered and squirmed in his arms. He wished he could see her responses.

"A fantasy. Something I can't touch in the light of day."

That was who he was. The shadow master. A man at home in the dark but not the bright light of day. "Then let's have this night."

"Can we?" she asked.

"You have to ask for what you want." He should stop flirting with her but couldn't help it. The heat of her body seared his skin and he knew he'd never be the same.

"I thought nothing was real here."

"Nothing is, except you and me." Since when had he ever been able to protect someone he cared for?

When had he ever been able to protect himself from someone he cared for? He knew then that he had to proceed carefully with Lynn. Despite the lust raging through his body he had to force his mind to take charge before it was too late.

"Then why am I trembling?" she asked.

He had no idea why. He shuddered because his control was razor thin and the only thing keeping him from stepping over the edge was the thought of losing the only family he'd ever felt a part of. "Because this is real."

"Is it?" she asked, pulling his head toward hers. He knew that the fantasy they'd woven around themselves couldn't last, wouldn't even withstand the faint light of dawn. But there was no power on earth that could keep him from tasting her again, from sating a thirst he'd never realized he had until he'd met her again.

He lowered his head, knowing this had to be the last time he gave in to temptation. But maybe just for tonight, he thought, he could forget reason and illusion. Forget Connelly and McCoy. Forget everything but this tempting woman in his arms.

The wine she'd consumed with dinner had to be to blame for the feelings coursing through her now. There was no reasonable explanation why she couldn't decipher between fact and fiction, but at this moment the line was blurred. She knew only that Seth looked real.

He felt real, too, strong and solid under her hands. His mouth against hers was more exciting than any she'd experienced before. She knew better than to trust her instincts where men were concerned. But she was a new bride and entitled to a wedding night.

Seth's mouth brushed against hers lightly. Just a breath of a touch. She forgot for a moment why Seth wasn't her forever man, because since he'd come back to Montana he seemed different. He'd certainly learned more about how to kiss a woman.

She longed for a deeper contact. Longed for his body pressed to hers. Longed for something she wasn't sure she should ask him for.

She parted her lips and skimmed her tongue over his bottom lip. He groaned deep in his throat—the sound primordial—sending shivers of awareness down her spine. She needed him.

He reciprocated, running his tongue around her mouth then dipping inside for a more intimate taste. He thrust deeply, claiming her for his own, not raising his head until she'd forgotten where they were.

He lifted her into his arms and swept her over the threshold. The room was dimly lit and the night seemed shrouded in fantasy. Never had she craved the chimera more.

"Don't wake me up if this is a dream," she said, not realizing she'd spoken until Seth set her on her feet in the bedroom.

Cupping her jaw in his large hands, he said, "I won't."

The words sounded like a promise. But she knew better than to believe a man's word when he held her in his arms. Seth's words sounded true, but in her heart she knew they weren't.

Seth walked to the windows and pulled back the draperies. Their twentieth-floor room was filled with the lights of the city. They illuminated Seth's profile. He seemed tough and alone as he stood there staring down at the street and lights.

He didn't move, just stood there. "Seth?"

"I don't want to force anything on you, Lynn."

She walked to him. His spicy masculine scent assailed her. "You aren't."

"I need you tonight," he said, the words raw as if torn from someplace deep inside him.

"I need you, too," she said, and knew those words for the truth they were.

He started to say something else, but she covered his mouth with her palm. "Enough talk. I'm ready for some action."

His eyes widened above her hand. He carefully bit the fleshy part of her palm, which still covered his mouth. The touch sent the forerunners of desire through her body, making her realize how much she wanted him.

She knew she wasn't the most attractive woman in the world, but when he touched her like that, his eyes dancing over her with a heat that could burn, feminine awareness flooded her and she knew that she was meant to be with him.

She pushed his tuxedo jacket off his shoulders. It hit the floor with a swish. He raised one eyebrow but she only smiled seductively at him and removed his bow tie. The studs on the front of his shirt were next, and when she reached his waistband she didn't hesitate.

She slid her hand down the placket of his pants, feeling the zipper beneath her fingers and the masculine hardness underneath.

He sucked in a breath and held it. She fondled him through the cloth of his trousers. Never had touching a man excited her so much. Languidly, she popped the snap at his waistband and slowly slid the zipper down.

"You're killing me," he said between his teeth.

"I know," she replied with a small grin.

She removed the remaining studs from his tuxedo shirt and stood back. A small wedge of masculine chest was visible between the parted edges, revealing tanned skin and a light dusting of hair. His opened pants defined his erection. She shivered, realizing that this sexy, virile man was hers for the night.

"Come here, vixen, and finish what you started," he said.

She returned to him and he pulled her close, bending to take her mouth in a kiss so deep and carnal, her mouth melted into his, and it was impossible to tell where one of them began and the other ended.

A hollow longing pulsed through her—the need to be filled with him, the compulsion to be connected to him in every way imaginable.

He caressed her back, releasing the side zipper of

her dress as he went. He lifted his head. "I've been wanting to do this since I first saw you in this."

Tugging on each sleeve, he pulled the dress away from her body and let it pool at her feet. She should have felt awkward, standing in front of him in heels, thigh-high hose and white lace panties, but the warmth in his eyes kept those feelings at bay.

He ripped his shirt off, flung it to the floor and pulled her to him. His chest was warm and solid against her. The hair stimulated her nipples. He kissed her again, his body moving against hers in need.

He pushed her back on the bed but didn't follow her. Instead he stood above her, watching her body in the shadows. She felt exposed. Her nipples were hard and her panties damp. She wanted him so badly that the separation made her feel vulnerable.

"Scoot back," he said.

She did as he asked.

"Stretch your arms out to each side."

"What are you going to give me if I do it?" she asked, to even the odds.

"Pleasure beyond your dreams."

She positioned her arms as he'd asked. He knelt on the bed over her, one tuxedo-clad leg on either side of her nylon-covered ones. Resting on his haunches, he touched her from crown to panties and back again, first with his gaze, then with the lightest brush of his fingertips. It was just a teasing caress that was gone before she realized it was there, all the way down her body to the waistband of her underpants.

Then his mouth took over. The wet heat engulfed her and had her writhing on the bed. She was consumed by him. Surrounded by him. Taken to another plane where only the two of them existed.

He dropped love bites on her neck and then he reached her breast. He paused and she glanced down at him. Her nipple was a firm berry right next to his mouth. His mouth was so close she could feel each exhalation over her aroused flesh, but still he made no move to take her into his mouth.

"Seth?"

"Waiting heightens the pleasure," he said. He was right, but she felt as if she was going to explode.

She lifted her arms and clasped his head in her hands. His hair was rich and luxuriant. Arching her body, she brushed her nipple against his mouth. He resisted at first but then with a moan, opened his lips and sucked lightly.

His touch assuaged the immediate hunger she felt, but then an even stronger one built in its place. He suckled her so strongly, as if he was finding a sustenance that only she could give him. She slid her hands down his back, burrowing her fingers under his pants and briefs, to caress his backside.

He treated her other breast to the same caress, then leaned back and blew softly on each. Her nipples tightened painfully.

"Seth, I need you."

"Soon," he promised. He continued his journey down her body, his tongue tickling her belly button and his teeth nipping at her stomach. He traced the edge of her panties with his lips and then pulled them down her body with his teeth.

When he reached her feet he watched her again. Lynn's hands moved restlessly on the bedcover and her body writhed, needing to be filled by him.

Seth stood and pushed his pants and briefs off in one motion. He grabbed a condom from the night-stand and quickly sheathed himself. He climbed onto the bed from the bottom and slid carefully up her body. His heat enfolded her before his limbs did. He held her so closely that she felt protected by him.

Then his mouth took hers and she felt ravaged, plundered, as if all her secrets were revealed to him. She wanted—no, needed—to back away from him, but he left her nowhere to turn except his arms.

He touched her with passion that demanded she respond to him. And she did, arching off the bed into the touch of his fingers as they stroked her most feminine place. "You're so beautiful when you blossom. Do it for me again now that I can feel it."

He found the bud that was the center of her desire and pressed in a circular motion with his thumb. He inserted first one finger into her body then a second. Returning to her breast, he suckled with powerful motions, and she was powerless to resist the tide that rose in her and swept through her.

His mouth and hands worked in harmony and brought her out of herself. Her entire body tightened and she cried out as pinpoints of light danced beneath her eyes. Then she clung to Seth, urging him up and over her. Needing him to meld with her. Needing him to fill her. Needing him to be vulnerable in the same way she was.

He raised himself slightly from her. She held his shoulders and realized that sweat covered his back. He'd paid a price for his restraint. Slowly he entered her, an aching inch at a time. His eyes met hers and once he was fully seated, he leaned down, his pectorals resting against her breasts, his mouth against her neck and his hands entwined with hers. He rocked slowly, building the fire in her again with each thrust of his hips.

He pulled all the way out with each thrust and then slid home. His mouth left her neck and he thrust his tongue deep into her mouth. The rocking motions of his body, the thrusting of his hips and tongue swiftly built her to the pinnacle again.

She arched frantically against him, searching for the release only he could give.

"Come on. Together this time," he said.

His hands left hers and he grasped her hips, holding them still for his thrusts. They went so deep she felt as if he'd touched her soul. When she again climbed to the stars, she knew that he had too, as pinpoints of light flashed behind her eyes and his groan of completion filled her ears.

Eight

Seth woke to the bright sun spilling in the windows and the phone ringing in his ears. The pillow next to him was empty, and he heard the shower in the distance. He grabbed the phone and answered it.

"Connelly," he said.

"It's Dad. I got your message, what's up?"

His father had a tone of voice that always made him feel as if he was being called on the carpet and without fail sent him back to those first weeks when he'd arrived at the Connelly household. "I got married last night."

His father sighed. "To whom?"

"Lynn McCoy."

"Are you sure about this, son?"

Seth thought about it carefully. Grant rarely called him son. He never knew how to take his Dad.

"Her ranch was in danger of foreclosure. I couldn't let that happen. The McCoys are like family to me."

"I understand."

"How's everything back home? I'd like to stay in Montana for a few more weeks but I can fly back to Chicago if you need me to."

"No need for that. Enjoy your new bride."

"It's not that kind of marriage, Dad."

"I didn't realize there were different kinds."

"There are. How's Charlotte Masters doing?"

"Rafe has Charlotte living with him to protect her and her baby. He told us that he's the baby's father."

His brother was going to be a father. Somehow that news made Seth long for things he knew he'd never have. "Dad, I'm sorry for my family's part in this mess."

"It's no more your fault than it is mine," Grant said.

Seth wondered if his father ever regretted having a son with Angie Donahue; if he ever regretted the affair that had brought Seth to life. Those thoughts were a big part of the reason why Seth had left Chicago. And only after he knew the answers would he feel comfortable returning.

He said his goodbyes and hung up the phone only to realize that the suite was very quiet. Rolling over, he saw Lynn standing in the doorway leading to the bathroom. She wore the thick terry robe provided by the hotel.

He smiled at her but she didn't smile back.

"Uh, that was my dad."

"I heard."

"How long were you standing there?"

"Long enough to be reminded that this is an illusion," she said, turning away and closing the bathroom door behind her.

"Dammit, Lynn. I didn't lie to you."

She didn't answer. He got out of bed and went to the bathroom door and tried the handle. It was locked.

"Come out and let's talk about this."

"As soon as I'm dressed."

"You're covered in that robe."

"Not enough."

"What's that supposed to mean?"

"Whatever you take it to mean, Seth. I just don't want to encourage intimacy between us."

"There already is intimacy between us."

"No there isn't. That was lust, Seth. Plain old-fashioned lust."

"Don't say it as if it were gone."

"Believe me it is."

He stalked to the bed and pulled on his pants. He wished the door wasn't between them.

"What happened this morning?" he asked quietly through the door.

"I heard you say it's 'not that kind of marriage.' What kind of marriage is it?"

"It's a business arrangement."

"Where we sleep with each other? Because that makes me feel cheap."

"No, it's not that at all. Lynn, come out so I can see you."

"No," she said. He heard the sound of tears in her voice and cursed himself for the bastard he was.

He'd known better than to give in to the temptation that was Lynn but had anyway and now he'd pay the price. And so would she. "The last thing I wanted was to hurt you."

"You warned me when we got here."

"That wasn't just an illusion last night."

"But it was. I'm tired of Las Vegas, Seth. Can we go home?"

"Yes," he said. He'd give her anything to make up for the hurt he'd unwittingly caused.

Lynn had never thought a few hours could feel so long. But by the time they landed in Montana she was more than ready to interact with other people, even if it was only the skycap who collected their bags. She tipped him while Seth went to get the car.

She shivered as she stepped outside. A cool breeze blew, making her wish she had a heavier jacket on. A light dusting of snow was falling and Lynn tilted her head back to watch it. Around her, people hurried and a cool breeze blew, but she only watched the snow, knowing soon the land would be covered in a pristine white that made it look innocent.

But despite what she'd always believed, she knew that innocence once lost could never be reclaimed. Her anger at Seth was superficial. She was really angry with herself. Watching the snow, she knew that she'd tried to keep him from realizing how much of herself she'd revealed.

But there'd been something in his eyes on the plane that made her realize he knew how vulnerable she was right now. And so he was treading lightly.

The Jaguar coasted to a stop in front of her and the trunk popped open before Seth got out of the car. She started to lift her bag but Seth glared at her. "Get in the car, Lynn."

She realized she may have gone too far earlier and wished there was some way she could go back in time and stay in the shower longer. If she hadn't overheard Seth's conversation, she'd still believe her hasty marriage could last.

But time travel wasn't an option. Besides, Lynn was a big girl. This wasn't the first time she'd taken a gamble on a man and come up empty.

"I'll admit that I haven't always been at my best with you," Seth said as he climbed into the car and put it in gear. "But I've always treated you with respect."

"Yes, you have."

He nodded and concentrated on his driving. She realized she'd offended his honor. This man was so complex, she thought. She knew that if she pushed hard enough she'd find a man who could love; knew that if she was willing to take the risk, Seth Connelly could be her dream man. But she wasn't sure she was tough enough to reach his heart without being hurt in return. One thing was for certain: she owed him an apology, but wasn't sure where to start.

"Hungry?" he asked after twenty minutes had passed. She stared at his profile. She could maintain her anger or get over it. And when she thought of the future, she didn't want to imagine her and Seth fighting.

"A little."

"I think there's a fast-food joint up ahead. Feel like cardboard burgers and cold fries?"

"That's fine.... Seth?"

"Yes," he said without looking at her.

"I overreacted this morning."

He pulled the car onto the shoulder and put it in park. "No, you didn't."

"Yes. I shouldn't have been eavesdropping and I certainly shouldn't have jumped to conclusions where you're concerned. You're a family friend who's done me a tremendous favor."

"I'd like to think I'm more than a family friend."

"Are you sure? Because earlier when you spoke to your father it didn't seem that way."

"Things with my family are complicated."

"Does it have to do with why you came to Montana in the first place?" she asked. She tried to turn the conversation away from her, because, knowing that she meant nothing to Seth, she'd be mortified if he realized how much he meant to her.

He nodded.

"Tell me. Is there anything I can do to help?"

"I doubt it," he said.

She recoiled, knowing she'd been tricked again. Knotting her hands on her lap, she promised herself this was the last time. How many times was she going to play the fool before she wised up? "My mistake."

His hand covered both of hers on her lap. "I didn't mean it that way. Damn, I'm no good when it comes to talking, but believe me when I tell you that it isn't you."

"Then what is it, Seth?"

"My mother has betrayed the Connellys once again. She's part of the Kelly crime family and she set my family up. This time involving me in her scheme."

"I'm sorry," she said. Her heart ached. The last thing Seth should have done was take on her burden of the ranch and now this marriage. He had enough problems of his own. Over the years she'd heard little about Seth's family, knowing only that he was the illegitimate child of a wealthy man. But she didn't realize the implication of being a child of that union.

He rubbed her hands in an affectionate gesture. "Thanks. But it taught me something that I should have already learned."

She waited. But he didn't speak. She glanced up at him. "What did you learn?"

"That I'm not meant for love."

"Don't be silly."

"I'm not. I believed my mother's lies when she came to see me, and good people were put into danger—even a pregnant woman. How am I supposed to handle the fact that I wanted so desperately to believe my mother wanted a relationship with me that I overlooked certain half-truths she told?"

"She's your mother. Of course you want to believe the best in her."

"Women lie," he said.

Her heart stopped for a minute. His words revealed something she didn't even realize he was hiding. It wasn't just his mother he didn't trust, or her, but all womankind for the betrayal that had started in his youth.

"What about your sisters?"

"They do it, too."

"I haven't lied to you, Seth."

He shook his head. She knew he couldn't trust her. She'd hurt him; he'd hurt her. Together the only thing they'd done right was their lovemaking, and even that had turned into a mistake.

She shook her head. "Let's go get that food you promised me."

"I don't want to leave this unsettled between us."

"One of us is going to have to trust the other for our relationship to change."

"I do trust you."

"To leave you someday," she said.

He didn't respond, only put the car back in gear and pulled back onto the desolate highway. In her heart she knew what she had to do if she wanted Seth Connelly in her life. She had to teach him that love wasn't a minus, but the biggest plus you could have on your side.

They arrived at the ranch just before lunchtime. There were three pickups in the yard; voices spilled from the windows of the bunkhouse and a new herd of cattle roamed the pasture. One lone cowboy wandered in from the range and headed for the bunkhouse.

"Where did all these people come from?" she asked.

"I hired them. Isn't it nice to see the ranch full of life again?" Seth asked as he helped Lynn from the car.

She shouldered her own bag and led the way to the house. Using her key, she opened the front door and was met by the scent of simmering stew. The hardwood floor under their feet had been polished and a new runner led the way to the stairs.

"But what's going on?" Lynn asked.

"I made some arrangements to start the ranch back down the path to its former success, which included hiring a new housekeeper/cook. I've also hired back as many hands as I could and ordered more cattle. The few you saw when we drove up are just the first shipment."

She dropped her bag on the floor and stood in the sunlight that spilled through the glass pane next to the front door, hands on her hips. "Thank you for making these arrangements. But it'll be a while before we can afford these kinds of changes. I mean, the little I had saved up to pay the bank will only cover two hands' wages for a month."

Seth hung his coat in the closet and then helped Lynn out of her coat. She looked the way he always pictured her in boots, a western shirt and faded jeans that clung to her long legs like a second skin. He knew that after this morning she wouldn't let him back into her bed, but he longed to be there even though he knew that he'd made a tactical error in sleeping with her. His body didn't care about that, and he adjusted his stance to give his erection some room.

"You married a rich man."

She took the coat from him and hung it herself. "That doesn't have anything to do with the McCoy Ranch. I still intend to pay back the money I owe you."

"We're married now. There is no yours and mine, only ours."

"If we were really married, I'd be the first to agree to that. But we aren't."

"I have a piece of paper in my pocket that says differently."

"But you told your family it wasn't that kind of marriage."

"Are you going to remember that forever?"

"You said it this morning. I'm not going to fool myself again, Seth. You wanted a business arrangement and that's what we've got."

"Be reasonable. The ranch is too big for you to handle. I only want to help."

"I was getting by."

"And working yourself to death. I'm only helping you out until you get back on your feet. Give the changes I've made a chance. If you don't like them, I'll put everything back to the way it was."

"Are there more changes than cattle and ranch hands?" she asked.

She started walking through the house, pausing in the living room to take in the changes. Finally she reached the kitchen where the wallpaper had been replaced and a new countertop installed. The floor had been buffed and refinished. The room resembled the one from Seth's memory and he was pleased with the work that had been done.

Coming up behind her, he said, "I had some craftsmen come out and repair the house as well."

She pivoted to face him. "We were barely gone a day and a half."

He shrugged. He'd thought the changes would make her happy. In fact, he'd almost forgotten he'd made the calls before they'd left for Vegas. With fire in her eyes and her hair hanging down her back, she enticed him, but he knew better than to come close this time. He'd hurt her this morning and he had a feeling it would take a lot for her to trust him again.

"I get results," he said with a shrug.

"I didn't count on this. There's no way I can pay you back for everything you've done."

He crossed to her. "I'm not looking for repayment."

"This is what I was trying to avoid. Things are worse now than when we left for Vegas."

"Do you really believe that?" he asked, because this was the first time he'd reacted from the gut and he'd hoped she'd be pleased.

"I don't know what I think anymore. This is too much. I wasn't expecting all these changes. I'm not sure I belong here."

"This is the only place you do belong."

"What about you?"

"I haven't found that place where I belong but when I find it I'll do whatever is necessary to keep it."

"It would be easier for me to accept all the work on the ranch if I thought you were going to stay here."

"I can't," he said, knowing that if he remained he'd forget that Lynn couldn't be his forever and eventually she'd lie to him and he'd have to move on.

She shook her head. "I know. I guess I'm just cranky. I need some air."

Seth watched her walk away, wishing things could

be different but knowing they couldn't. If he was ever going to have a night's rest again, he needed to make sure that Lynn was safe and secure. He never wanted her to have to worry about losing the ranch again. And if it took every penny he had in the bank, then he'd use them.

Nine

Lynn walked out of the house as fast as she could. That Seth thought nothing had changed between them made her want to scream. But she didn't do the part of the enraged woman really well, so instead she settled for leaving before she said something she'd regret.

The changes in the ranch were alarming. But the barn was soothingly familiar with scents and sounds she'd smelled and heard since childhood. The barn was dim, scant sunlight filtering through the open door.

"Can I help you, ma'am?" said one of the new ranch hands.

"No, thank you."

"Name's Bill if you need anything," he said, and went back to the tack he'd been repairing.

She hadn't noticed him in the shadows, but the evidence of his presence was there in the room. She skirted by him, grabbing her tack and leaving quickly. She saddled Thor and mounted him.

Riding out of the barn, she felt her control slipping. She wished that Seth was really her husband so that she could talk to him about these changes. So that she could find a way to make him understand that she needed to be a part of the ranch, the way it was a part of her.

The hustle and bustle of the ranch around her told her she wasn't necessary to the daily chores, and that made her sad. Since Matt had left and her parents died, she'd been the lifeblood of this place, but suddenly she wasn't anymore.

Three ranch hands looked at her as she rode past them, each tipping their hats to her. Did they know she was their boss?

Was she, really? Or did Seth have something else in mind? She clicked to Thor as soon as they were past the last gate and he took off. Only when the wind was rushing through her hair and the sun beating on her neck did she let the tears flow freely down her face.

Thor stopped under a copse of trees near a small pond. It was her thinking place. She and Matt would sneak out here when they were children to talk and swim. It was, she realized as she dismounted, the place where she'd shared her first kiss with Seth.

She walked quietly around the tree, swamped by images of the past. She remembered the way things used to be but could never be again. Remembered Seth as a boy and now more intensely as a man. Her man, she'd thought. But maybe not.

The sound of a galloping horse got her attention, and she watched a rider approach from the same direction she'd come from. The man was tall with dark hair and no hat. She knew instinctively that it was Seth. Part of her—the girl who'd given her money to a con man—rejoiced at the fact that he'd followed her. But a more sensible part—the girl who'd been left with a bankrupted ranch—knew that he had to have a reason.

He slowed the horse to a stop in front of her and sat there watching her for a few minutes. The silence was uncomfortable but she didn't want to break it.

"Can I join you?"

She shrugged.

"I brought offerings with me."

He dismounted and began removing containers and a blanket from his saddlebags. He'd brought lunch, she realized.

She helped him settle the blanket on the ground under the tree, and they opened the containers of food. She set a place for them with the picnic dinnerware and cutlery he'd brought. Coming from Seth, this wasn't a ham sandwich and Coke picnic, but a wine, cheese, fruit and crackers meal.

He poured them both a glass of wine and then leaned back against the trunk of the oak that provided shade for them. "Want to talk about it?"

"The ranch?"

He shook his head. "Whatever is bothering you."

"I don't know where to start."

He just sipped his wine and ate a piece of cheese, waiting for her to find the words to tell him her troubles. Waiting for her to bare her soul to him. Waiting, it seemed, to rescue her once again.

"I don't like change," she finally said.

"I can understand that. But change isn't a bad thing, you know."

"For me it is. Every change that has happened in my life has brought about some sort of worsening circumstances."

"Remember the luck I was talking to you about on our wedding night?"

She nodded.

"I think your fortune is changing, Lynn."

"I feel so..."

"Scared? Alone?"

"Silly," she said.

"You could never be silly."

"Thanks. And I mean for everything you've done."

"I should have asked you first before I instigated so many changes."

"I would have protested."

"Arguing with you is half the fun," he said.

He stared up at the branches of the tree. A cool breeze blew through the air, causing her to shiver a little. He lifted his arm in silent invitation for her to join him. She slid closer to him, snuggling into the warmth of his body.

"I've visited this place many times in my memory," he said.

"We had some fun out here during those summers you stayed with us," she said softly.

"We did, but that's not why I remember this place," he said.

"It's not?" She hoped he remembered their first kiss.

"You know it's not. Childish pranks pale in comparison to a lovely blond-haired beauty."

"Oh, Seth."

"I've never forgotten that evening. The stars shone so brightly, your hair was free, like it is today, and you came into my embrace with all the eagerness and passion with which you do everything."

He tilted her face up to his. "I don't want you thinking I'm a bad change."

Before she could respond, he lowered his head, blocking out the sun. All she could do was respond to this man who'd already claimed her body. She had a feeling that her heart was next.

Seth lingered over her mouth but pulled back before things went too far. Not physically but emotionally. The changes that Lynn had spoken of were external ones, but he knew their marriage and intimacy had been just as hard for her to adjust to. "I didn't come out here to make love to you."

"You didn't?" she asked, all sassy woman, confident of her appeal to the man she was with.

"I wanted to see why you were out here alone. To make sure you weren't hiding."

"I wasn't hiding. Just running from the truth, I guess."

He knew what that was like. Though he wouldn't admit it to a soul, he'd been running since he was twelve. And he knew it deep inside. "Maybe I've given you a reason to stop."

"Am I reason enough for you to stop running?" she asked.

"What?" He scooted away from her, not sure what she was trying to ask him.

"You've been using this ranch in Montana as a place to hide from your family for as long as I've known you. Has it helped?"

He thought about it. His first instinct was to bluster around and make sure she knew that he wasn't running from anything. Cowards ran. He didn't.

"I'm not running," he said firmly. He wasn't about to let Lynn draw him into an emotional discussion. She was the one with the adjustment problems, not him. He was well adjusted, at least most of the time.

"My mistake. It's just when someone shows up

unexpected with hardly a bag packed, it might seem like he left unexpectedly…maybe when he sensed trouble.''

''Are you calling me a chicken?'' He reacted with anger—the safer of the emotions funneling through his body like a winter runoff out of control.

''Never. A person might see it differently if they didn't know you as well as I do.''

''Well, sweetheart, you need an updated lesson.'' He wasn't sure why she thought she could beat him in a war of words. He was a lawyer, words were his lifeblood.

''Teach me.''

He'd like to teach her something. She seemed so smug in her summation of his life. As if she knew everything there was to know about him.

''I doubt you could be taught.''

She leaned across the blanket and cupped his jaw. That one touch was so soothing, so intimate in light of their conversation that he shivered under it. He wasn't going to let her manipulate him.

''Tell me,'' she said. She was his own personal Siren sent to call him to the rocks.

And like a man, he followed the sweet sound of her voice and found himself talking about stuff he never discussed. Not even with his half siblings. ''I told you about my mother. You don't know what it's like to have to take responsibility for a mess your parent has made. To know that you helped make the mess because you hoped maybe this time she was sincere when she said she needed to be near her child."

She watched him with those big eyes, focusing so intently on him that the words seemed to flow from someplace deep inside where he'd always hidden them. "Then my dad sent me to military school. And it was so different from the world I'd known."

"Oh, Seth."

"No pity. I don't want that."

"I understand."

"You can't possibly, because you think I took the easy way out and left Chicago. But I couldn't stay. I couldn't let my mother use me against the Connellys."

"You wouldn't let yourself be used that way."

"I don't know. My mother, even though I see her infrequently, is still a big influence."

"How?" she asked.

"I've never understood why she left me with my dad when I was twelve."

Lynn crawled across the blanket and embraced him. She held him so close that Seth couldn't remember a time when she wasn't in his arms. Her scent—flowers and sunshine—surrounded him and made him feel safer than he'd ever felt. He'd never had security, but he'd created it for himself. And suddenly this woman, his wife, was showing him that what he'd created was only an illusion.

"Sometimes love means letting go," she said

softly. "Your mom probably saw a better future for you with the Connellys."

"I don't know. I think she tired of having to be responsible for another person."

"Could be. But I think it's time for you to let go of your mom and the past."

"I don't know if I can."

"Only you can decide. But remember that it took a lot for me to trust a man again."

"Me?"

"Yes, you. There's no one else I would have accepted help from."

"That's because I wouldn't take no for an answer."

"Details, details."

She led him to a safe middle ground, and he followed her willingly. But he didn't like the shift in power. Until this moment he'd been in control both of his life and their future. But something had shifted. And he was ready for it to shift back.

Leaning closer to her, he claimed her mouth again. He knew that one taste wasn't going to be enough to sate his thirst. And that scared him more than anything in his life ever had.

Having Lynn in his arms was more temptation than he could bear. Even knowing that he couldn't return to Chicago without her wasn't enough to keep him from kissing her. The touch of her lips was healing balm on his bare soul.

He didn't examine it too deeply. The blood rushing through his veins demanded he make love to her. Demanded he claim her as his woman. Demanded he take her now before she realized that he wasn't good enough to be her man.

The wind ruffled through the trees and a fish jumped in the lake. He absorbed all of these sounds with a feeling of timelessness. He wasn't Seth Connelly about to make love to Lynn McCoy Connelly. He was man about to claim his woman. Not for a moment, not for convenience—but for all time.

He wanted this moment to be a gentle merging of their bodies, a quiet affirmation of the bond their words had formed. But his soul cried out for immediate gratification.

His hands shook as he undid the buttons of her blouse. Today the sunlight bathed them. There were no shadows to hide in for either one of them. He stripped the clothing from her. With the light pouring onto the branches and dappling her skin, she was illuminated and he knew she was the most beautiful woman he'd ever seen.

The knowledge that she had so profound an effect on him humbled him and made him realize he must never let her have that knowledge.

The body he'd learned by touch he now learned by sight. She was exquisitely formed. Her breasts high and full, her stomach gently curving and the mound at the apex of her thighs covered with blond downy hair.

"I have to touch you," he said.

"Please..."

Starting at her neck, he claimed her for his own. As he swept his hands over her skin so much paler than his, she trembled under his touch. He bent and let his breath warm her skin, blowing gently on the curve of her neck, her breast, her stomach and her center. She shifted restlessly on the blanket.

"Do you want more?"

"Yes," she said.

"Then let me give you everything I am."

He started again at her neck, biting her flesh softly, then soothing her with a small lick. Her pulse accelerated and his own answered. Her skin was an addiction in itself: having had one taste, he couldn't get enough. He slid down, lingering over her full breasts, suckling them and teasing her until her hips left the blanket and her hands clutched the back of his head.

She urged him farther down her body and though his instincts screamed for him to hurry, to take the sweet nectar he'd drawn from her, his control was greater. As was the need to have tasted all of her. To have driven her beyond anything she'd ever experienced. To have made her his in a way that was so complete she'd never leave.

Her stomach and belly button were next and tasted as addicting as her breasts, but he was so close he could smell her arousal, and the need to taste her essence drew him lower. And then lower still until he was crouched between her spread legs.

He rested his cheek against her softness, heard the cry she tried to stifle and looked up at her. Her breasts heaved rapidly with each breath she took. Her hands moved restlessly from the blanket to her stomach and back again. Her hips undulated under him, and he lowered his head slowly.

"Lynn?" he asked, knowing that there was no turning back once he took her this way.

She grasped the back of his head and lifted herself to him. Nothing he'd ever been offered had he craved more.

"Touch me, Seth," she said.

He did. He parted her gently, laying bare the focus of her desire and then bent to lap at her with his tongue. She tasted like a woman—his woman.

She moaned deep in her throat, her hips moving more urgently now. He eased two fingers into her tight sheath and continued working his tongue against her. She gasped his name on each breath, and her hands had left his head, her fingernails digging into his skin with greater strength, until she thrust her hips high against him and cried out.

Her cries echoed in the wind, surrounding him. He didn't bother to remove his shirt or boots. He needed her flesh to surround his. He needed it now.

He freed his erection and thrust into her. He could feel her sheath still throbbing with her climax. Her arms surrounded his shoulders and her hips caught his frantic rhythm. He held her hips, slowing them down, knowing that the pleasure would be more extreme if they had to wait for it.

The small of his back tingled, sweat gathered on his chest and with each thrust her nipples teased him.

"Come on, Seth," she urged. "Faster."

"Not yet," he said between clenched teeth.

"Please..."

He slowed his thrust a margin more. She moaned and attempted to force him deeper. As a punishment he keep his next thrust shallow.

"What are you waiting for?"

"You."

"I don't want to go alone again."

He realized he didn't either. Lacing their fingers together, he glanced down into her eyes. He saw her soul staring back at him. He hoped his wasn't revealed to her.

"Now," he said and pulled completely out of her before driving heavily into her one last time. Buried hilt deep, he started to come. Her body tightened around him and she cried out again. Seth could only answer with her name.

Spent, he rolled onto his back and pulled her with him. They were still joined and he was reluctant to separate them. He pulled a corner of the blanket over them and they lay entwined until the cold and falling darkness drove them back to civilization.

Ten

"I had no idea it would get dark so quickly," Seth said as he rolled the blanket and placed the last empty container in his saddlebags. Twilight spread across the land as the sun dipped behind the mountains. The darkness wasn't total but she knew it wouldn't be long before it was.

"You've never visited in fall before," she said.

He nodded. A breeze ruffled the tree branches and she shivered a little. Winter was definitely on its way.

"Let's go home and sit in front of a fire," Seth said.

"Sounds good."

It sounded better than he could know. She hoped that Seth would find her house his home. That together they'd restore the ranch to its former glory, working together to make it successful, sharing a life filled with love and hard work.

But a part of her doubted he'd stay, knew that he planned to return to Chicago and acknowledged that he needed to. He had to resolve things with his mother and his family. But would he leave her a whole man and return to his family and summer vacations with Matt? Or would he leave her temporarily and return to make his home with her?

That uncertainty dulled the sweet sensations lingering from his lovemaking and the quiet serenity she'd felt being cradled in his arms. Too much was unresolved in their lives. She hoped she wasn't putting her heart in jeopardy by believing in something that didn't exist.

"Good thing the trail back to the house is on flat land," she said, hoping none of her doubts showed on her face.

"I wouldn't let anything happen to you," he said, tugging her to him and holding her so tightly she couldn't breathe. Surrounded by his warmth and his scent, she rubbed her nose against the collar of his jacket and tasted his neck.

"I won't let anything happen to you either," she said. Hope blossomed in her heart, that maybe this time she'd chosen a man who'd stay with her. He dropped a lingering kiss on her mouth.

"We'll have to do this more often," he said, taking a step back. But he held her hand as he led her to her horse. There was a sense of rightness to this time they'd spent together here. The secret she carried in her heart blossomed fully and she realized she loved Seth. Way more than she'd loved Ronnie, who'd taken her money and run for the West Coast. Way more than the land she'd almost lost. It was scary and exciting, humbling and exulting at the same time.

But the girl who'd been left alone wanted to believe that this time she'd found the real thing. But part of Lynn feared she hadn't.

"Will we do it again before you return to Chicago?" she asked, needing some sort of confirmation.

"Hm-mm." He kissed her again and she didn't feel secure by that nonanswer. Seth had said it before: he was a lawyer and he made his living playing with words. Why not use one now?

And why didn't she just ask him? She was scared of the answer but knew that not knowing was worse than his leaving. So she took a deep breath and asked what was on her mind.

"Seth, are you still planning to leave?" she asked, looking up into eyes that were as dark as the land around them.

His fingers tightened on hers and she knew that he wasn't sure. Somehow that lack of security coming from Seth made her feel better.

"I'm not sure," he said.

"That's not the answer I'd like to hear."

"Baby, I know that. It's just...I don't know."

She nodded. It was something. Actually it was

more than a little thing. She knew that Seth was beginning to realize the truth of love. That was why he didn't know where the future would take him.

"Let's go," he said, boosting her into the saddle and mounting his own horse.

Seth moved with the surety of someone raised around horses, though he hadn't been. She knew it was the summers he'd spent here that had given him that confidence and knowledge. It reassured because if he'd retained his horseman's skills, surely he'd retained the other thing her family did very well—love.

Seth was quiet on the ride back. Twilight darkened around them, and shortly the house came into view. It was as if fourteen years had been erased. She remembered the summer Seth had kissed her. They'd done everything together that year: rode the herd, swam, and spent hours talking under the very tree where they'd just made love. She'd felt as if she'd found her true love. But she knew she'd been wrong before. Was she this time?

In the bunkhouse the hands were settling in for the evening meal. Lynn wasn't sure who'd be waiting for her in the house. The barn was empty when they entered, which relieved her.

"Does the housekeeper spend the night?" she asked.

"No, she drives in from town. Her hours are nine to five, but you can change them if you want to." Seth dismounted and started removing his horse's tack.

"Why would I do that?" she asked, doing the same herself.

He took her saddle from her, carrying it to the tack room. "She works for you."

"I don't want to be her boss. I want to work the land and take care of my stock."

"Baby, you don't have to do any of that anymore."

"What do I have to do?"

He scooped her up in his arms and carried her toward the house. "Just keep loving me."

His words echoed what was in her heart, but she had a feeling he was referring to something physical, while what she wanted to give him was more than her body. It was her heart and soul. And she was very afraid he already owned them.

His words echoed in his head and he knew that he had to distract her before she realized just how much of his soul she'd claimed. Her weight was insubstantial as he carried her through the yard and bounded up the stairs, but the weight of her trust and emotions weighed heavily on him. For the second time in his life he felt out of control and he didn't like it. He'd have given anything to know how to handle Lynn.

The world was spinning farther and farther away from his comfort zone. He was a mover and shaker in Chicago but here in Sagebrush he was a man at the mercy of one small woman. And he hoped she'd never know it. But there was a gleam in her eyes as she watched him that let him know she had a glimmer of realization.

He hadn't planned to make love to her again and without protection. But knowing that he had sealed his fate. He wasn't going to be able to divorce Lynn. In retrospect, the thought of marrying her and leaving her down the road hadn't been a good plan.

He shifted her weight to open the door. The sconces in the hall had been left on, creating an inviting glow. He set Lynn on her feet and helped her remove her jacket, hanging it with his in the hall closet. She stood a few feet from him, illuminated in the glow. She looked ethereal and he felt very human and big and bulky in her world.

The house felt the same way it always had except now it also felt like his home. Never in any of the houses he'd dwelled had he ever really felt home. Except here. He remembered his first night here only days ago, when he'd been hesitant to enter, and now he knew why. Somehow he must have sensed that he wouldn't be able to leave Lynn or the McCoy Ranch easily.

He hesitated, seeing the dark shadows of furniture in the parlor. Lynn had a lifetime of memories to surround herself in. Seth had always felt as if he was running from the past. Lynn had a family that had always supported her and taught her to believe in herself. Seth didn't know what support and love were until he was twelve.

Lynn chuckled as she turned her gaze the same way.

"What are you laughing at?"

"You and Mama's footstool."

Seth smiled. Then he realized that he would have to make a piece of furniture for her. He didn't have any idea how to start. He wasn't even sure what to get for her.

"Are you making me something?" he asked. Maybe she wouldn't, considering the business aspect to their marriage.

"What?" she asked.

"Your family tradition—the furniture. Is there something you're making for me?" An awkward feeling spread through him. Maybe he should have kept his mouth shut.

"What do you think?" she asked, suddenly serious.

Damn. Now he felt naked in front of her. If he said yes, she'd know how important it was to him that she treat him as a real husband. And if he said no, he was afraid he'd hurt her feelings. "I don't know."

"Why not?"

Double damn. Now he knew he should just pick her up and carry her upstairs. When she was writhing under him in bed, she didn't ask questions that cut through his armor and pierced his heart. "I'm not sure you want me to stay."

When she closed the distance between them and

cupped his jaw in her hands, he felt soothed to his troubled soul. ''Oh, Seth. Of course I do.''

He stared into her eyes and saw the truth of her words revealed there. He held her tighter, feeling the fragility of her bones under his embrace. He was so much stronger than she was, but there were times when he knew he was the weaker one.

''Show me.''

She nodded and took his wrist to lead him into the darkened parlor. He followed her willingly, realizing that the hold she had over him was stronger than the hold he had over his willpower. Suddenly the sweet seduction he'd been wallowing in changed in timbre and he knew he couldn't let Lynn take the lead.

''I'll show you,'' he said, sweeping her into his arms and carrying her up the stairs. He shouldered open the door to his bedroom. The room was bathed in moonlight through the open draperies on the windows. The full-size bed was neatly made, and his laptop glowed in the darkened room.

He laid her lightly on the bed and began unbuttoning his shirt.

''Stop, Seth.''

''Why?''

''I want to do this my way.''

He felt vulnerable to her because of their conversations. Letting this woman who meant so much to him make love to him was out of the question. He needed to wrest back control from her, to reaffirm his place as the leader in their relationship.

"I—"

She knelt on the bed and tugged him down beside her. "It will be painless, I promise."

She forced him to lean back and brushed his hands aside, opening his shirt and pushing it off his shoulders. She tugged it down but stopped before he could free his arms. He was trapped or at least he let her believe he was.

"Comfy?"

"Not really."

"You just need to trust me."

"If you didn't have that devil gleam in your eyes, I might be able to."

When she leaned down and nipped at his pectoral, the touch of her teeth on his flesh zapped him straight to his groin. He moaned and reached for her, only to find his hands shackled by his shirt.

"Like that?" she asked.

"Oh, yeah."

"Still not sure you want to be here?"

"Being here was never the issue."

"Control was," she said. "Surrender to me, Seth. I'll keep you safe."

In the end he had no real choice. She seduced him with quick nibbles of his flesh, with hands that searched out each of his pleasure points and lingered on them, with eyes that caressed with a caring that made him ache to possess her. And finally when he was ready to surrender anything she asked, she moved over him and took him deep in her body.

They moved together as if they were made for each other, and before long they shot to the stars—together. As they drifted slowly back to earth, Seth held her as closely as he could and knew that he'd glimpsed heaven with this woman. He prayed for the first time since he was twelve years old and standing in the opulent foyer of his father's mansion. And his prayer had the same desperation now as it did then.

Please, God, let this be real and not a dream.

Lynn woke shaken and alone and intensely vulnerable. The pillow next to hers was cold, telling her that Seth had been awake for a while. It was seven-thirty, past time for her to be up and doing the morning chores.

She dressed quickly and hurried downstairs to find coffee waiting, breakfast on the table and Mrs. Stuffings in charge of the kitchen and house. Lynn hurried outside to the barn, only to find that the men had taken over that space.

For the first time her home wasn't hers.

What was Matt going to say when he returned home? The ranch was as much his as it was hers. She'd done everything in her power to save it, but now the reality of her actions was that Seth had more or less taken control of it. She felt cut off from her own land.

Snap out of it, girl, she told herself. The land was still hers. Just her role on it had changed.

At loose ends and with nothing to do, she sought

out Seth and found him ensconced in her father's old den. Seth looked right sitting behind the oak desk, a piece her great-grandfather had made.

His laptop was plugged in, and a slim printer was spitting out papers. Seth talked into his cellular phone while typing something into the computer.

He looked up when she entered but motioned for her to give him a minute. She glanced around the room. The floor-to-ceiling bookcases held books that had taught generations of her family to read. As she skimmed her finger past the titles, she saw an old carpentry book that her mother had used to make the footstool in the living room.

She really needed to get to work on a piece for Seth. But what did he need? And would he be staying to use it? If she made him a new desk, he could use it wherever he went. She made a mental note to stop by the lumberyard that afternoon.

Her route around the room took her to the large bay windows that overlooked the pasture and barn. The ranch bustled with activity, and despite her earlier thoughts, she knew that she'd done the right thing by marrying Seth. As much as she didn't like the disruption of her routine, she knew this change was for the best.

Seth patted her on the butt and tugged her down onto his lap. He was still talking softly into the phone. She leaned into his warmth and for a minute felt the sense of rightness for which she'd been searching a lifetime. She knew that Seth was the man she was meant to spend her life with and wondered if she'd be strong enough to let him go when the time came.

Part of her knew that he could never make his life here in Montana. He was a lawyer, a big-city mover and shaker whose entire affluent family waited for him in Chicago. She was a small-town working-class girl who didn't want to leave the splendor that was Sagebrush. She needed the fresh air, snowcapped mountains and open spaces to survive.

When the quiet rumble of his voice stopped, she looked at him. He winked at her.

"Seth?"

"Almost done, honey," he said, still clutching the phone to his ear.

As much as she enjoyed sitting on his lap, she felt restless. Clearly Seth wasn't going to have time to go for a ride with her any time soon.

She glanced at the clock and realized she had about thirty minutes until her shift at the diner. She hadn't quit her job yet and she welcomed the distraction it provided. She scooted off his lap.

Seth covered the mouthpiece of his phone. "Where are you going?"

"To town. I'll be back later."

"We need to talk," he said.

She nodded and turned toward the door.

"Don't I get a goodbye kiss?"

"You seem rather busy."

"I always have time for you," he said.

She bent toward him, intending a swift kiss, but

when their lips met, Seth took over the embrace. Setting his phone on the desk, he cupped her face, tilting her head so that he could thrust his tongue into her mouth. The kiss was deep and carnal, and when he lifted his head, her breath wasn't steady.

He tugged her back into his lap. His erection nudged her hip and she knew that if she waited for him to conclude his call they'd be back in bed. Tempting though that was, she knew she needed to be more to Seth than a bed partner. She needed to be a contributing partner.

She took his face in her hands and kissed him with all the love that was welling in her heart. Kissed him as if it were the first time their lips met and as if it were the last time. As if all time had stopped around them and nothing but he and she existed in the world.

Then she dropped her hands, caressed his arousal that strained against his inseam and walked toward the door.

"Honey," he called, "give me ten minutes and I'll meet you upstairs."

Though she knew she shouldn't, Lynn nodded and went back upstairs to his bedroom. But ten minutes came and went and when it reached thirty, she grabbed her purse and headed for the diner. It seemed that Seth didn't need her as much as she needed him. And though she tried to pretend it was anger coursing through her, she knew it was also hurt. The kind of hurt that only love could heal.

And Seth had already told her he wasn't a man who'd ever love again.

Eleven

Seth cursed the situation with his family. Both sides of it. The Connellys were riding a string of bad luck that had to end soon. And his mother's family seemed to be responsible for every bit of it. He was going to have to go back to Chicago soon. But Lynn's words echoed in his mind.

You can't keep running from your problems.

Thinking of Lynn soothed the savage part of his soul that was torn between two families. He hurried up the stairs, hoping she was still waiting for him. But it had been forty minutes since she'd left him alone and wanting her.

When he found his bedroom was empty, he optimistically checked the one that used to be hers, but it was empty as well. He hurried downstairs but couldn't find her anywhere.

"I think Mrs. Connelly took her truck and headed toward town," Mrs. Stuffings said. "This came for you a few minutes ago."

She handed him an envelope from the banker, Mr. Cochran. It held the deed to the McCoy Ranch. A feeling of rightness filled him. Despite the way he'd started out in life, he realized he'd become a good man. And a month ago he wouldn't have been able to acknowledge that.

Lynn had given him something irreplaceable and he was glad he'd been able to save her ranch for her. He went back into his office and wrote a brief note to make sure she understood the ranch was hers. Then knowing there were some words he could never say out loud, he wrote them instead on the note.

He went upstairs and put the envelope on her pillow. Then he grabbed his keys and went out to the Jag. He took a quiet pride in the way the ranch was starting to take shape. It was beginning to resemble the memories he had of it. He'd left a message for Matt, at the base where his outfit was stationed, updating him on the situation with Lynn. He expected to get a call about thirty seconds after Matt read it.

If Matt had suddenly married one of his sisters, Seth knew he'd call Matt and demand to know what the hell was going on. Seth realized he was going to have to have a better explanation for Matt than "I did it to save your ranch and repay your family." Matt wouldn't buy that. He'd know there was more to it than that.

Seth wasn't sure he was ready to admit there was more to his marriage than he'd revealed to Lynn.

Lynn's truck was parked behind the diner on Main Street. Maybe she was visiting friends, he thought. She'd seemed kind of restless earlier.

He hoped she didn't resent him but knew she probably did. Hell, he'd be ticked off if someone had taken over the way he had. But Seth knew he was a man of action. He didn't like to sit around when he saw a way to change things.

He pulled his car into the parking lot and realized he'd chosen the same spot he'd had on the first night he'd arrived in Sagebrush. How had she become so important to him in such a short span of time?

He couldn't believe how much had changed since then. Yet at the same time his relationship with Lynn had always been a part of him. There was a sense of rightness to it, as if fate had always meant for them to be together.

Frankly that frightened him. Almost as much as the soul-shattering lovemaking they'd shared the night before. He felt the same desperation he'd experienced every time he'd depended on his mother.

Though he believed in carving his own destiny, a part of him wondered how long Lynn would stay with him. Common sense said he'd be the one to leave. But he didn't know how long she'd stay with him.

His feelings for Lynn were stronger than any he'd

ever experienced with another woman. And though he'd always balked at fear and faced danger head-on, he knew love made him weak. These soft emotions she inspired in him made him weary.

He sat in the car staring into the diner. Lynn wasn't visiting with friends. She was working, he saw. She smiled at a couple in a booth as she poured them coffee.

He felt her slipping farther and farther from his grasp. The fragile hold he had on her was weak and he knew it. Bonds of the flesh weren't strong enough to hold a woman like Lynn. But showing her how he felt was a risk he couldn't take. There had to be some way to convince her that he was worthwhile without revealing how deeply he needed her in his life.

He climbed from his car and walked inside the diner. She glanced up as the door opened, her eyes weary as she watched him. It seemed his rotten luck with relationships was holding. He'd managed to put her on guard.

On the positive side she didn't seem that angry with him for standing her up earlier. But as she drew closer, he realized he was mistaken. Hot emotions glittered in her eyes, and he thanked God they were in a public place. Otherwise he had the feeling Lynn would have let him have it.

"Table for one?"

"I was looking for you," he said.

"You've found me."

"Yes, I did. And not for the first time."

"I wasn't running from you."

"I know. That's not your style."

"No, but it is yours."

That zing cut to the bone. It never paid to let anyone close. "Can we have a civil conversation?"

"Yes. I'm sorry. Not enough sleep last night."

"I'd gladly give up all my restful nights to spend every night with you."

"Would you?"

He nodded. "Can you sit down and talk to me?"

"Let me put this coffeepot down and get one of the other girls to cover for me."

He took a seat in the booth he'd been given his first night in the diner, though the anxiety in him now was so much more intense than it had been that first night. He had so much more to lose than he'd had before. Before, he'd been running from his own shame in his mother's actions. Because he'd desperately wanted her love and ignored what his gut had told him. Now, he realized, he was here because of his own.

Lynn slid onto the bench seat across from him. Resting her elbows on the table, she leaned in. "I've only got ten minutes so we'll have to talk quickly."

"You don't need to work here. Why don't you give them your notice? I'll take care of you."

She sighed. "I don't want you to solve all my problems. I've been working all my life and it's too late for me to stop now."

"Maybe you can find pleasure in being a wife. You used to work on the ranch and enjoy it."

"There's nothing for me to do there anymore."

"There will always be stuff for you to do."

"I can't sit around. I need to know that I'm contributing to society. You should understand that."

"I'm trying to."

"I appreciate all you've done for me. I feel like Cinderella after she's been swept away by Prince Charming. But the reality is, Cinderella wouldn't have been happy sitting in the castle the rest of her days and doing nothing. And neither am I. I have to know that I'm not just an ornament on your arm."

"Honey, you are more than that."

"Don't speak so quickly, Seth. I was in the house this afternoon when you made certain promises and then didn't deliver on them."

"Lynn—"

"I understand that business comes first but I can't just wait around until you have time for me."

"I know. I apologize. We can figure out something for you to do."

"Like what?"

"I don't know. Not working as a waitress."

She shook her head. There was a deep sadness in her eyes that spelled doom for his tender heart. A heart he'd hidden behind a shield of cynicism and weariness but one that she'd reached regardless.

"I don't think this marriage is going to work," she said.

"Yes, it can." Damn, did he sound desperate?

"What makes you so sure?" she asked.

Come on, guy. Bare your soul, he thought, realizing he couldn't he tell her a partial truth. It was, after all, the reason he'd originally married her.

"The debt I owe your family is too high for me to allow this marriage to dissolve."

"Are you saying you married me to repay my family?" she asked in a hoarse voice.

He knew he'd made a tactical error. He'd made them a time or two in the courtroom but this was only the second time he'd made one in real life. The first had resulted in the endangerment of an innocent young woman. This second one held consequences too harsh to examine.

"Yes, I did."

"Well, I guess it's safe to say I now understand why this marriage of convenience has been so important to you."

Lynn stared at the man she thought she knew and realized once again that she'd fallen for the illusion. In real life there was no Prince Charming on a white horse that was going to save the Cinderella from a cold, lonely life. Reality was that Prince Charming would use his money to make her life easier, and her heart would remain locked away—forever.

What had been blossoming in her heart as love had been nothing more than a game to him. She felt little and foolish. Every bit the small-town hick to his big-city sophistication.

She'd fallen for a guy who'd promised her the world once before. At least Seth hadn't paved the way with pretty lies. He'd done it with sincerity and integrity, but he'd done it all the same. When all was said and done, she'd be alone and heartbroken again.

This time she had no one to blame but herself. Even Seth had warned her not to be tricked by the smoke and mirrors. But her heart was easily duped. And it had led her once again to an intense vulnerability.

The power Seth had over her made her weak as she realized she didn't wield the same strength over him. Her hands trembled, and for a moment she couldn't breathe. She laced her fingers together and squeezed until the shaking passed.

"Lynn, are you okay?" hc asked.

She closed her eyes and tried to pretend that he wanted more from her than— What exactly had he wanted from her? It wasn't her family's land or her money. He'd wanted to absolve himself from some lingering feelings of gratitude left over from a lifetime ago.

The backs of her eyes burned, but she refused to let her tears fall. She wasn't that weak. She would never let him see how deeply he'd hurt her.

She shook her head and glanced around the diner. Anywhere but at the man who'd made a place for himself in her life with a network of deceptions. "I'm fine."

"I didn't mean that—"

Staring down at her clenched fingers, she searched for words that wouldn't reveal how deeply he'd cut her. She searched for a way to deal with the emotions rocketing through her at superspeed. "I know exactly what you meant. I'm your penance."

"You are *not* my penance."

"Well, it sure as hell seems like I am. Either that or your punishment."

He shoved his hands through his hair and looked to her like a man caught. She knew that she'd come close to the truth but she'd never be able to discover it on her own. He had to trust her enough to tell her.

That, she realized, was something he'd never do. Seth had been betrayed by the women that he'd depended on too many times for him to ever really trust her. And without trust they had nothing.

"Why did you have to make it feel real?" she asked, finally looking at him.

His eyes seemed haunted as he rubbed the bridge of his nose. Her instincts urged her to soothe him. He'd been working nonstop since they returned from Vegas—was it only a day ago?

"It wasn't an intentional thing," he said. "I've tried to be as up front as I could."

But his words reminded her that there was more to Seth Connelly than met the eye. He played his cards close to his vest and from their time in Vegas she knew he played to win.

"You've never sounded more like a lawyer. Omission doesn't absolve you."

"I'm not trying to be absolved."

"Look me in the eye and tell me you weren't using me to assuage your guilt for the past."

He wouldn't. Instead he placed his large hand over her clenched ones. The hand that had caressed her body to heights she'd never experienced was now a touch she could not tolerate.

She unclenched her hands and slid them out from under his grasp. Glancing up, she saw that his gaze was shuttered. He'd revealed more emotion the first night he'd come into the diner when he was still a long-lost friend to her than he showed tonight after he'd become closer to her than her breath.

"I can't," he said at last. The words told her that there was no future in her relationship with Seth.

She started to slide out of the booth but he stopped her.

"Neither of us was looking for a love match," he said. "This is a situation that lets us both have what we want. You have the ranch, I have the knowledge that I've finally done something for the McCoy family that has worth."

"What about me?" she asked, knowing she had nothing left to lose.

"I don't follow," he said.

"I'm more than a means to an end," she said more loudly than she'd intended.

His gray eyes were diamond hard and she wished there was a way to get him to release the emotions he kept bottled inside. "I know you are."

"Then why did you use me?" she asked at last. She could understand his wanting to repay her family. Heck, she knew she'd never have a moment's peace until Seth was repaid for what he'd done for the ranch. But making her his wife in body if not in soul had crossed a line.

"I never did. You needed me and I came through for you. I solved your problems and restored your home."

She had needed him, but she hadn't realized she'd been so transparent. He'd given her back something uniquely feminine that she'd lost when Ronnie had taken her money and left her. "I didn't ask to be rescued."

"No, you didn't but you needed to be."

She couldn't admit to that. She may not have been wildly successful on her own but she hadn't been a total loser. "I was doing okay."

"I beg to differ. Anyway, you left me no choice."

"How did I do that?" she asked. Why didn't she just get up and walk away? There was no way they were going to ever come to an agreement. Not until her heart had time to mend. Maybe they could meet again in thirty years and she'd be able to forgive him for making her fall in love with him.

"I couldn't let you lose the ranch."

"Well, I appreciate that, Seth, I really do. But why did you have to make it personal?"

"Emotions have nothing to do with the ranch."

"Don't they have anything to do with us?"

"You know they do. I want you more than any woman I've ever dated."

"I'm not talking about lust."

"Neither am I."

"I wish I could believe you."

"Why can't you? You've trusted every two-bit con man that's come through town. Why can't you trust me?"

"I do trust you," she said.

"Sure you do, honey. You trust me to disappoint you like every other man in your life."

"Matt has never let me down," she said.

"Maybe not intentionally but he wasn't here when you needed his strength and advice."

"I don't blame Matt for this."

"I'm not saying you should. My point is I've never let you down."

Feeling vulnerable, she lashed out. "It's hard to trust a man who doesn't trust himself."

Lynn's words cut deep to a part of himself that he'd hidden away for a long time. He stopped trying to make peace with her. "You don't know what you're talking about."

"Maybe, but it seems to me that a person who

takes to the road when things get tough isn't someone who trusts himself to survive the situation.''

He grew very still. He wasn't sure where she was going with this conversation, he only knew that her words made him realize she saw through the trappings of wealth and education to the tough street hood who still lived underneath.

''Are you calling me a coward?'' he asked.

She shook her head then tilted it to one side, her eyes piercing his, and he knew she saw all the way to his soul with that gaze. ''I guess I am.''

''No man would still be standing if he said that to me.'' That was the tough little boy who'd learned to fight before he entered school. The rough kid who'd thought nothing of picking pockets or shoplifting. The wild teenager who'd stolen a car to prove he was a man and then had his father teach him there was nothing manly about bravado.

''I'm not insulting you. You are a brave and honorable man when it comes to work and strangers, but once it gets personal, you put up barriers, and if that doesn't work then you leave.''

He knew that she was trying to protect herself, the same way he was. Could they ever find a way to live together in this intense vulnerability they seemed to generate in each other? ''I haven't left you.''

''Telling me that emotions have nothing to do with our relationship is the same as running away. Until you trust yourself you'll never be able to love me.''

''Why do you want my love?'' he asked.

"Oh, Seth…"

He stared at her. Her big violet eyes were wide and glassy like spring pansies wet with rain. And he knew that he was the cloud that had rained on them. "I want your love because I love you."

For a minute a sense of relief washed over him. It was right that she loved him. But he knew that it wouldn't last.

He wished he could believe her. But love didn't work like that. He'd seen his father who professed to love his wife cheat on her. He'd seen his mother who professed to love him use and betray him. He'd seen other women whom he dated profess to love him only to leave him when they realized he was a working man with a working man's values.

Truth was a paramount value for him, and when he saw the hope glistening in those eyes he knew he had no choice.

"No, honey, you don't," he said as gently as he could.

The color left her face as she stared at him. "I thought trust was our problem, but now I know it isn't."

"Then what is?"

"Your lack of humanity. Because no man who's shared what we've shared—the joining of our souls and the deep conversations—no man whom I've let see my dreams could look at me and say I don't love him."

She stood up and yanked off her apron with vicious

movements that betrayed more than her anger. ''I feel sorry for you because no matter how far you run you'll never find a home until you acknowledge that you love others and are yourself lovable.''

He said nothing. He'd never be that weak. He'd seen love destroy stronger men than him. He'd seen what people did in the name of undying affection and he wasn't going to be victim to that.

She shook her head and walked out the door of the diner. He watched her leave with a certain sense of inevitability. He'd known she'd go someday. He'd hoped she'd stay longer but he wasn't surprised she'd left.

He realized the customers in the diner where staring at him, so he put on his tough-guy face and shrugged.

''Want some free advice, partner?'' asked a gnarled cowboy seated across the aisle from him.

''Not particularly,'' Seth replied. ''I've found advice to be worth what you pay for it.''

''Well, son, this one's on me. Go after that girl and tell her whatever she needs to hear. Or one day you'll wake up and realize the mistake you made in letting her go and it will be too late.''

Seth knew the man was right. ''I... Thanks.''

''No problem. I wish someone had said the same thing to me years ago. Then maybe I wouldn't have only horses to keep me company.''

Seth liked the old cowboy. He wasn't looking for sympathy and there was something about his attitude that reminded Seth of himself. "You looking for work?"

"Most ranchers won't hire an old saddle bum like me."

"I'm not most ranchers. Stop by the McCoy Ranch and tell Buck, the ranch foreman, that Seth Connelly sent you."

"I'll think about it," he said and went back to eating his meal.

Seth walked outside. It was a crisp cool day. He shoved his hands deep into his pockets as he walked to his car. He got in but didn't start it.

He had two choices, and he had to be honest—pointing his car east and heading back to Chicago was the safest thing he could do. But he couldn't leave until Lynn told him to go.

He wasn't going to walk away from her or the home he'd found with her until he'd given their relationship one more try.

He told himself it was because she liked the silences he fell into so often. He told himself it was because she was sexy and flirty and could turn him on with the most innocent look from under her lashes. He told himself that it was because she listened to him talk about the past and didn't judge him.

But he refused to acknowledge the real reason even to himself. He only knew that a life without Lynn in it wasn't one he wanted to live. He only knew that Lynn and he had a bond that went deeper than time or location. He only knew that he'd never be able to walk like a man again if he didn't convince her to stay with him.

He started the car and pulled out of the parking lot, hoping he'd be able to make his peace with Lynn. But her words came back to him from that afternoon they'd made love under the tree.

Sometimes love means letting go.

He hoped he was strong enough to let go of her if necessary, but a part of him realized they were meant to be together. He only hoped he could convince her of that.

Twelve

Lynn pulled her truck to a stop in front of the house she'd lived in her entire life. But she didn't get out. Her face was wet from crying and she didn't want to go inside and see the housekeeper. She wiped her face and watched a man walking around the house. She realized he was a housepainter and that he was restoring the finish that she'd never had the time to.

Seth was a man capable of such generosity that she knew he had to have a heart. If only he could trust himself to love.

But she knew that life had taught him hard lessons. That didn't excuse him for not being able to realize the gift they had been given, but it made his actions more understandable.

She was no stranger to heartbreak, but this time…oh, this time it felt as if she'd never recover. Slowly she exited her pickup and as she closed the door she saw the stenciling on her truck: McCoy Ranch—Home Of The Best Beef In Montana.

Seth had given that back to her. He'd given her the seed to make the future as glorious as the past had been. She went inside and heard the housekeeper in the kitchen. She didn't want to talk to a woman she hardly knew so she quickly went down the hall to the den.

The room wasn't hers anymore and she sensed Seth's presence as clearly as if he were in the room with her. She walked slowly to the desk where he'd been working this morning. She ran her fingers along the back of the executive-style desk chair where he'd sat.

Leaning forward, she rested her cheek against the back. The scent of his cologne lingered, and she had to close her eyes against a longing so deep that she knew she'd never really be free of it.

Never had she found a man who'd put up with her the way Seth had. He'd actually seemed to like her feistiness when most men could barely tolerate it. Never had she found a man who'd listen to her dreams and desires and then make them come true for her because he wanted her happiness. Never had she found a man she felt safe enough loving.…

And she'd managed to drive him away.

Her encounter with Seth at the diner had made her

realize she needed to talk to her brother. She couldn't spend the rest of her life trying to protect those she loved by keeping things from them. Before she could change her mind, she found the card Matt had given her before he left, and dialed the number.

A stranger answered and she asked for her brother. Matt was unavailable but they'd have him call her. She felt better for her actions and knew she should have gone to him long ago for help. Being independent was fine, but asking for help when she was in over her head wasn't a bad thing.

She knew that was what Seth had taught her. Even if they didn't find a way to make their marriage real, she'd always be glad he'd shown her the value in having another person help you with your problems.

The thought of never seeing Seth again made her want to curl into the fetal position and never get up. Instead she decided to do something. She ran her hand along the scarred wooden arms of the chair. Suddenly she knew just the piece of furniture she'd make for Seth—not a desk but a new desk chair so that he'd be surrounded by the love he didn't believe she could have for him whenever he was working.

If he didn't come back to the ranch she'd send it to him in Chicago. The love she had for him was too strong to be broken by anger. She might even have to leave the ranch if he proved stubborn and didn't return to her.

But leaving the ranch no longer frightened her the way it used to. Living alone was what she feared. And if they weren't together, she knew that she and Seth would never find true happiness.

She decided to get changed before heading out back to the carpentry shed and starting on Seth's chair. As she entered her bedroom, she glimpsed herself in the mirror and realized that she wasn't a quitter. She'd never given up on anything.

Seth Connelly had better be prepared for the battle of his life if he returned to Chicago instead of to the ranch.

There was an envelope on her pillow and she recognized Seth's bold masculine handwriting on the outside. It was just her name.

She opened the large manila envelope and pulled out two papers. The first she recognized as the deed to the McCoy Ranch. The second was a folded piece of paper. Slowly she opened it up. Her heart was in her throat as she forced herself to see what he'd written.

It occurred to her that Seth didn't have to return to the ranch now. She knew that he'd accomplished what he'd set out to do: rescue her and her ranch.

Lynn,
Enclosed is the deed to the ranch. I hope that we will be able to make your ancestral lands into the home I've always been searching for.

Seth

They were simple words that could mean anything, but Lynn knew Seth well enough to look beneath the surface. He wasn't going back to Chicago, she realized. Unless she'd chased him away by telling him he lacked humanity.

If she had, she knew she'd go after him, because the man who'd written this note was a man who could love her for all time. A man who felt things that he could never say. A man who needed to have a home to come to when he was weary of battle.

She knew that his life with his families was a battle for him at times. A torn allegiance to the woman who had given him birth and the man who had fathered him. A torn allegiance to the people who'd taught him to survive and the people who'd given him a reason to. A torn allegiance between what he was given and what he craved—a real family.

She bit her lip and knew that the chair would have to wait. She had to find Seth now. She ran down the stairs and threw open the door—only to crash into Seth. Their heads knocked together and stars danced in front of her eyes.

He caught her close and she leaned into him, knowing she'd found in this man the love that had always eluded her. But how was she going to make him see that it was just the thing he needed?

Seth was afraid to let go of Lynn. She'd come through the door like a woman with a mission. She felt right in his arms. His head ached from where their heads had bumped but he didn't mind the pain.

It was proof that she was really in his arms. Never had the embrace of another person been more important to him. Never had he needed that human contact more than right now. Something new had sprung to life inside him on the drive to the McCoy Ranch, and the change wasn't finished yet.

All he knew was that he intended to make sure that she stayed with him. That she didn't give up on him yet. That she took the opportunity fate had given the both of them.

He'd broken all speed limits to get back here to her. And now that he was here he didn't know what to do. He knew the words she wanted from him, but the one time he'd muttered those words his mother had patted him on the head and left him in a stranger's home.

"Are you okay?" he asked. Her eyes were wide and vulnerable. A faint wetness lingered under her eyes, and the knowledge that he'd made her cry made him want to curse.

Despite the circumstances of his birth he'd always tried to rise above what he'd been born as. But looking at Lynn's wet eyes, he acknowledged he really was a bastard when he wanted to be. Hurting Lynn, the one woman he'd always wanted to protect, made him realize that he needed to change.

"You've got a hard head," she said lightly. But the attempt at levity cost her, and she had to look away from him. They'd both said too much earlier and not enough.

He wiped the wetness from under her eyes. She flushed a little and he knew she'd hoped that he wouldn't know he'd made her cry. "I'm sorry."

She nodded.

"I mean it, honey. You gave a precious gift and I rejected it."

She closed her eyes. Was it too late? he wondered. Had he killed the love she'd professed to have for him? Was there a way to keep her by his side without showing her how deeply he needed her there?

"You were right about me. I've never been able to trust that I was worthy of anyone's affection."

"But you are. I wish I could show you that."

"I did a lot of thinking after you left," he said, trying to find the words to tell her what was in his heart.

He noticed the paper clutched in her hand and realized she'd opened the deed and the note he'd left for her. He dropped his arms and stepped a few feet from her. It took all his control not to turn and get back into his car. Not to drive away as fast and far as he could. Not to leave her while she held the most vulnerable part of him in her hands.

"I see you opened my note." *God, please don't let me screw this up.*

The shrewd look in her eyes worried him. He wished she'd tell him again that she loved him. It would make everything so much easier. But then again, easy things weren't always worth having, he thought.

"You are a fraud, Seth Connelly."

"How do you figure that?" he asked, again worried he might say the wrong thing.

"You love me. You might not know it, but this piece of paper proves it."

Seth froze, feeling much the same as he did that first night in his father's home: afraid to move or breathe in case he broke something. He'd come so close to hurting Lynn, he'd already made her cry today. He knew that his rough edges wouldn't disappear overnight—hell, they might never go away—but he knew that for Lynn he was willing to try to soften them.

Despite his designer suits, fancy car and penthouse apartment, he was still at heart a street punk who wasn't good enough for this woman who had a generous heart.

He clenched his hands to his sides, still not sure what to do. The tingle in his gut that had started in his car when he'd realized that he couldn't live without Lynn now spread throughout his body. His ears buzzed.

Lynn closed the space between them and wrapped him in her arms, holding him so tightly he thought she'd never let go. He wanted her to never let go of him. She cradled his head in her hands and looked up at him.

"Tell me I'm wrong," she said.

He unclenched his hands and slid them up the back of the woman who'd come to mean more to him than life itself. Her breasts nestled against his chest. He hardened against her and knew that if he took her to bed, he'd be able to show her easily that she was right. But she wanted words.

"No, you're not wrong."

"Can you say the words?"

"The last time I said them I was wrong."

"When was that?"

"To my mom when she introduced me to my father."

"Seth, my love isn't like hers. Mine is a love that isn't going to end or change even if you can't ever say the words."

"Are you sure?"

"Yes, I am."

He knew he had to tell her the truth that was in his heart but couldn't here or now. The sun shone on them, making him feel more exposed than if he'd been in the dark.

"Where were you hurrying to?" he asked.

"To find you."

Her words made his heart beat faster and he knew that whatever the future held they'd be together. He scooped her up in his arms and carried her into the house.

"Where are you taking me?"

"To bed. I might not be able to tell you how I feel but I damn sure can show you."

Seth placed her on the center of the bed and lowered himself to her. He kissed her with the passion she'd come to crave from him, thrusting his tongue deep in her mouth until she forgot the individual tastes of each of them and they were only one.

He undressed her with ease and surety, and within a minute she was lying naked in front of him. He stood to disrobe, his eyes never leaving her body. She felt like the sexiest woman alive in that moment. The fire in his gaze started one that pulsed through her with the beating of her heart, pooling in the center of her body.

The cotton quilt on the bed felt soft under her naked hips and she stretched her arms out, beckoning him to her. He crouched at the foot of the bed and moved up slowly, caressing her from her feet to her legs, stopping at the mound of her femininity.

Instinctively she tried to close her legs.

''Don't,'' he murmured and settled himself between her legs.

He parted her tender flesh and lowered his head to taste her, dropping first soft, light kisses on her most sensitive flesh and then as her hips began to rise to meet him, using a stronger touch on her there.

He slid two fingers inside her and she clenched her body around them. Being filled by him was pleasure but she wanted more. She wanted his hardness to fill her. She needed him to be with her at this moment.

''Come to me,'' she said.

''Not yet. This time is for you.''

He lowered his head again, this time to suckle at

her breasts. She felt voluptuous as his hands and body brought her close to the edge of climax. His mouth left her nipples to slide once more back down to her center and this time when he touched the bud of her desire she went over the edge.

She shivered in his arms as he moved over her. His chest rubbing against her breasts and torso. His mouth nibbling on her neck. His hands clutching her buttocks and that hard, hot part of him seeking entrance to her body.

She opened herself to him, wrapping her legs around his waist as he slid inside her. He buried himself so deeply that she finally felt as if they'd become one.

He moved slowly, building her once again toward climax and this time as her nerve endings began to quake she called out his name.

"I love you," she said, gazing deep in his eyes.

He thrust into her with more and more urgency, his eyes never leaving hers, and he shouted his climax. She held him in her arms as they slowly drifted back into themselves.

His head rested on her breast, his breath tickling her nipple. She imagined they'd spend the rest of the day and night here in bed. Life, she realized, had a way of giving you exactly what you needed. Though a part of her would always want to hear the words from Seth, he did a wonderful job of showing her how he felt.

"Thank you," she said.

He rolled to his side, carrying her with him and settling her head onto his shoulder. "I should be thanking you."

"Why?"

"For all of this," he said, indicating the house around them.

"I wouldn't have my house to share with you if you hadn't stepped in."

"I might have given you back your ranch, but you've given me a gift that I never knew existed."

"What was that?" she asked.

"The knowledge that life is empty no matter how many possessions you own. Life is meaningless unless you have someone to say those three little words to you."

He leaned closer to her, held her so tightly to him that she couldn't breathe and whispered in her ear, "I love you, Lynn."

Tears burned the back of her eyes and she whispered back. "I love you, too."

They spent the afternoon making love and talking about their plans for the future and knew in their hearts that they'd been given a second chance to find happiness.

Epilogue

Lake Shore Manor, the Connelly home in one of Chicago's finest neighborhoods, was an overwhelming sight to Lynn.

"I don't belong here," she whispered to Seth as they stood in the marble-floored foyer.

"Yes, you do," Seth replied, kissing her.

"Why are you so sure?" she asked.

"Because you are by my side and finally I feel like I belong here."

She smiled at him and Seth knew that he and Lynn had really completed each other.

"Come inside, Seth," said his father. "The family is waiting for you."

"Dad, this is Lynn, my wife." A quiet sense of

pride filled Seth as he said the words. He'd never wanted a spouse, but having committed his life to Lynn had filled him in places he'd never realized he'd been empty.

"Welcome to the family, Lynn," Grant Connelly said, embracing her. Watching his dad and Lynn chat, Seth realized that his father had welcomed him the same way when he'd arrived. His father's heart was a big one and had room for every one of his children and, as the family continued to grow, their spouses.

"It's good to be home," Seth said.

"I'm glad to hear you say that," his dad said.

"Emma, Seth's here."

Emma Connelly still looked regal and glamorous despite her sixty years. She embraced Seth, and for the first time he realized that he had a mother who loved him and she'd been here all along. He didn't know how to tell her that but there was a glimmer in her eye that told him she already knew.

The family was waiting for them in the formal living room. He introduced Lynn to his sister Tara, and the two of them got along very well. He knew they would.

His brother Drew, who was speaking on the phone despite the cacophony around him, walked forward to embrace Seth in a welcoming hug. He held out the phone. "Daniel's on the phone."

He took the phone from Drew, eager to speak to his eldest brother who'd claimed the throne in Altaria almost a year ago.

"Congratulations, Seth," Daniel said. "I can't wait to meet your new wife."

"Thanks, Daniel. I never thought I'd marry or settle down."

"It's amazing how the right woman can change your life."

"You can say that again. How are things in Altaria?"

"Life would be better without a Gregor Paulus—the man's driving me crazy. Is it possible to fire a royal retainer?"

"Are you asking me as a lawyer?"

"Nah, just venting to you as a brother," Daniel said. "Is Dad nearby?"

"Hold on."

Seth finally felt equal to the task of being a Connelly man. As if he'd found his home and his place within his family. He passed the phone to his father and rejoined Lynn.

She was chatting with his sister Maggie, who seemed upset. "You okay, Maggie?"

"I'm just worried about Lucas Starwind," she said.

"Why?"

"At Tom Reynolds's funeral he seemed so enraged. I don't know if he was angry with himself or the fact that Tom died while investigating our family's case. I just wish I could help him deal with all of that pain."

"Some things a man has to work out for himself."

"I know that."

"Don't do anything impulsive, Maggie. Let him be."

"I will," she said in an unconvincing tone. "I barely know him."

Seth gazed at his sister, wondering just how deep her concern for Starwind ran. He hoped she wasn't getting in over her head. He'd heard that the other man was a tough-as-nails P.I. who preferred to keep to himself.

Lynn slipped her arm around his waist and he let his worries for his sister melt away as she left them to get a drink from the wet bar.

"So this is your family," she said softly.

"Yes," he said. "My family. I guess I just didn't feel like I belonged until I had you."

"Really?"

He nodded. He bent close to kiss her, thanking fate for the twice-in-a-lifetime chance he'd been given with Lynn and his family. He knew that this time he wouldn't push it away, because the gift was too precious to turn aside.

* * * * *

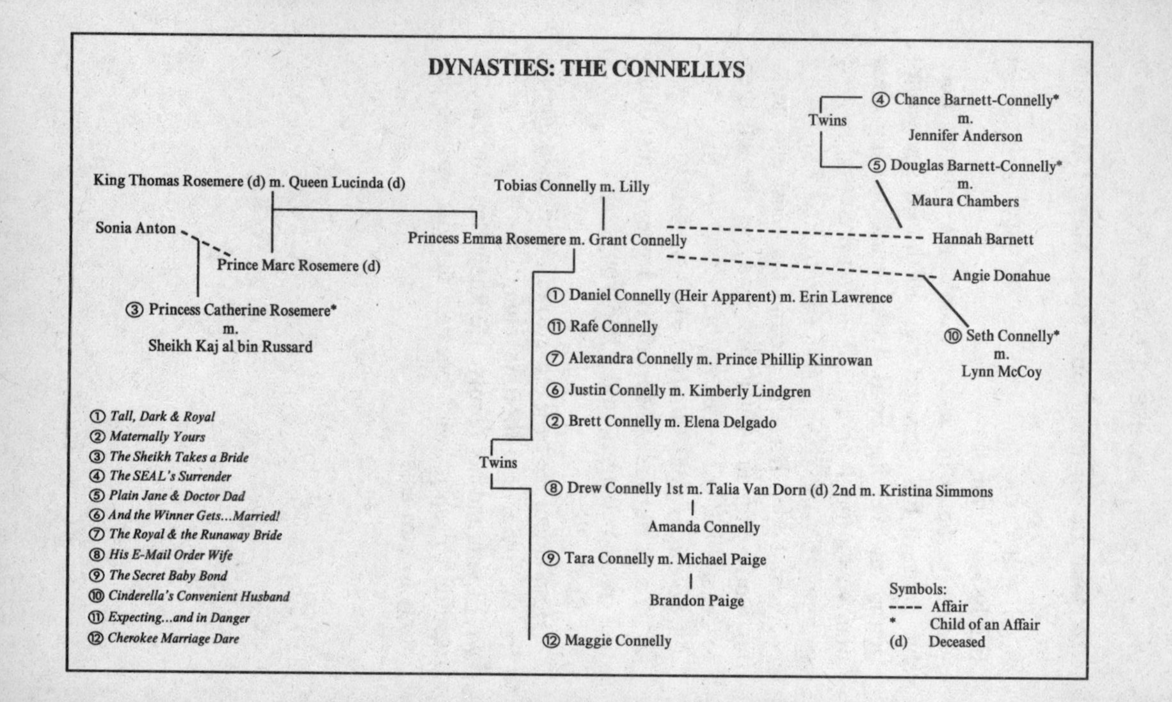
DYNASTIES: THE CONNELLYS
King Thomas Rosemere (d) m. Queen Lucinda (d)
Sonia Anton
Prince Marc Rosemere (d)
③ Princess Catherine Rosemere*
m.
Sheikh Kaj al bin Russard
Tobias Connelly m. Lilly
Princess Emma Rosemere m. Grant Connelly
Twins
④ Chance Barnett-Connelly*
m.
Jennifer Anderson
⑤ Douglas Barnett-Connelly*
m.
Maura Chambers
Hannah Barnett
Angie Donahue
⑩ Seth Connelly*
m.
Lynn McCoy
① Daniel Connelly (Heir Apparent) m. Erin Lawrence
⑪ Rafe Connelly
⑦ Alexandra Connelly m. Prince Phillip Kinrowan
⑥ Justin Connelly m. Kimberly Lindgren
② Brett Connelly m. Elena Delgado
Twins
⑧ Drew Connelly 1st m. Talia Van Dorn (d) 2nd m. Kristina Simmons
Amanda Connelly
⑨ Tara Connelly m. Michael Paige
Brandon Paige
⑫ Maggie Connelly
① Tall, Dark & Royal
② Maternally Yours
③ The Sheikh Takes a Bride
④ The SEAL's Surrender
⑤ Plain Jane & Doctor Dad
⑥ And the Winner Gets...Married!
⑦ The Royal & the Runaway Bride
⑧ His E-Mail Order Wife
⑨ The Secret Baby Bond
⑩ Cinderella's Convenient Husband
⑪ Expecting...and in Danger
⑫ Cherokee Marriage Dare
Symbols:
---- Affair
* Child of an Affair
(d) Deceased

DYNASTIES: THE CONNELLYS

continues...
Turn the page for a bonus look at what's in store for you in the next Connellys book—only from Silhouette Desire!

#1472 EXPECTING...AND IN DANGER

by Eileen Wilks
November 2002

One

The Windy City was living up to its name the second time someone tried to kill her.

At least, Charlotte thought they'd tried to kill her. Sprawled across the hood of a parked car, with panic pounding in her chest, her hip throbbing, her calf burning and her coat flapping in the wind, she couldn't be sure. Maybe the driver simply hadn't seen her.

"You all right, lady?"

She stirred and looked up at the concerned face of a tall black man with a gold ring in his nose, another in his eyebrow, a leather jacket and with a Cubs cap on his shaved head. Several others had stopped on the busy sidewalk to stare and exclaim. She caught snatches of conversation—"crazy drivers!" and "must have been drunk" and "where's a cop when you need one?"

Not here, thank goodness, she thought. The last thing she needed was to draw the attention of the police.

"I'm fine," she said to the concerned and the curious. "Thank you for asking." She pulled herself together mentally as she climbed off the car. Her knees weren't sure of themselves, but after sorting through her aches, she concluded she wasn't badly hurt. The car had missed her, after all. Thanks to the wind.

Charlotte had been crossing the street—with the light, of course. She always crossed with the light. She'd finished her bagel two blocks back and had been holding on to the sack, which was destined for the next trash can. A strong gust had grabbed it right out of her hand. She'd turned, meaning to chase it down so she could dispose of it properly. And had seen the car.

It had been headed right for her in spite of the red light that should have protected her. It had even seemed to speed up in that split second between the instant she'd seen it and the next, when her body had taken over and hurled her out of its path.

But maybe that was paranoia speaking. Although it wasn't really paranoia, was it, if there really were people out to get you?

''You sure you're okay?'' the man in the Cubs cap and nose ring asked.

She put a hand protectively on her stomach. A little wiggle inside assured her that all was well, and she drew a deep, relieved breath.

Her backpack. Oh, Lord, she couldn't afford to lose that. Where—? Kneeling, she spotted it halfway under the car and dragged it out. Her arms felt like overcooked spaghetti.

''Hey, you want me to call someone to come get you?''

It was the Cubs fan. ''Thank you, but that won't be necessary.'' Standing with the backpack slung over her shoulder was a good deal harder than it should have been. Her knees weren't in much better shape than her spaghetti arms.

Surely it had been a freak accident.

''Better sit down a minute. You're pale as a ghost. Bleeding, too.''

Irritation threatened to swamp good manners. She hated being fussed over. ''I'm always pale. I'll take good care of the scrapes at work.''

''You got far to go?''

''Just up the block, at Hole-in-the-Wall.''

He cast a dubious glance that way, which she perfectly understood. The restaurant was aptly named, an eyesore in an area that had once been solidly blue-collar, but was skidding rapidly downhill. The neighborhood was seedy, a little trashy, not quite a slum...everything she'd fought so hard to leave behind.

"You ain't up to working yet," he informed her with that particular male brand of arrogance that scraped on her pride like fingernails on a chalkboard.

"I appreciate your concern, but it isn't necessary." She started limping down the sidewalk, hoping he would get the hint and go about his own business.

It didn't work. He kept pace with her. "Don't trip over your ego, sister. I'm not hitting on you. Don't care for teeny, tiny blondes with big mouths." He shook his head. "You sure talk fancy for someone who works at the Hole. Smart-mouthed, too," he observed. "Why you working at the Hole?"

"For my sins." Which was all too literally true. But she was going to get things straightened out soon, she promised herself for the fortieth time. Somehow.

* * * * *

COMING NEXT MONTH

#1471 All in the Game—Barbara Boswell

She had come to an island paradise as a reality game show contestant. But Shannen Cullen hadn't expected to come face-to-face with the man who had broken her heart nine years ago. Sexy Tynan Howe was back, and wreaking havoc on Shannen's emotions. She was falling in love with him all over again, but could she trust him?

#1472 Expecting…and in Danger—Eileen Wilks

Dynasties: The Connellys

They had been lovers—for a night. Now, five months later, Charlotte Masters was pregnant and on the run. When Rafe Connelly found her, he proposed a marriage of convenience. Because she was wary of her handsome protector, she refused, yet nothing could have prepared her for the healing—and passion—that awaited her in his embrace….

#1473 Delaney's Desert Sheikh—Brenda Jackson

Sheikh Jamal Ari Yasir had come to his friend's cabin for some rest and relaxation. But his plans were turned upside down when sassy Delaney Westmoreland arrived. Though they agreed to stay out of each other's way, they eventually gave in to their undeniable attraction. Yet when his vacation ended, would Jamal do his duty and marry the woman his family had chosen, or would he follow his heart?

#1474 Taming the Prince—Elizabeth Bevarly

Crown and Glory

Shane Cordello was more than just strong muscles and a handsome face—he was also next in line for the throne of Penwyck. Then, as Shane and his escort, Sara Wallington, were en route to Penwyck, their plane was hijacked. And as the danger surrounding them escalated, so did their passion. But upon their return, could Sara transform the royal prince into a willing husband?

#1475 A Lawman in Her Stocking—Kathie DeNosky

Vowing not to have her heart broken again, Brenna Montgomery moved to Texas to start a new life—only to find her vow tested when her matchmaking grandmother introduced her to gorgeous Dylan Chandler. The handsome sheriff made her ache with desire, but could he also heal her battered heart?

#1476 Do You Take This Enemy?—Sara Orwig

Stallion Pass

When widowed rancher Gabriel Brant disregarded a generations-old family feud and proposed a marriage of convenience to beautiful—and pregnant—Ashley Ryder, he did so because it was an arrangement that would benefit both of them. But his lovely bride stirred his senses, and he soon found himself falling under her spell. Somehow Gabe had to show Ashley that he could love, honor and cherish her—forever!

SDCNM1002